HOUSE OF THE ANCIENTS
& other stories

Also by Clifford Garstang

Fiction
In an Uncharted Country
What the Zhang Boys Know
The Shaman of Turtle Valley

Fiction, as Editor
Everywhere Stories: Short Fiction from a Small Planet
Vols I, II, III

HOUSE OF THE ANCIENTS

& OTHER STORIES

Clifford Garstang

Press 53

Winston-Salem

Press 53, LLC
PO Box 30314
Winston-Salem, NC 27130

First Edition

Cover image, "Colorful house exterior in India,"
Copyright © 2018, licensed through iStock

Cover design by Claire V. Foxx

Author photo by Miscellaneous Media Photography

Library of Congress Control Number
2020930601

Printed on acid-free paper
ISBN 978-1-950413-18-8

for my parents, again

Acknowledgments

The author thanks the editors at the following publications where these stories first appeared:

Bound Off, February 2008, "Last Call"

Bourbon Penn, No. 5, September 2012, "American Marsupial"

Cagibi, No. 3, July 2018, "Downhill"

Gargoyle, No. 70, Summer 2019, "Pluck"

The Hopkins Review, No. 12.4, Fall 2019, "The Scottish Play"

Joyland, May 2012, "Cousin Barnaby is Dead"

LitNImage, Summer 2011, "The Open Book"

Los Angeles Review, Vol. 7, Spring 2010, "Justice, Inc."

Neworld Review, Vol. 12, No. 84, 2019, "A Fire in Winter"

Northville Review, March 2011, "In Hoan Kiem Lake"

Parhelion, No. 1, April 2018, "Lost in Translation"

Per Contra, Winter 2009, "In the Palace of Cortés"

Potomac Review, No. 42, Fall 2007, "Sophie, Sophia" (as "Nicky, Natalia")

Predicate, July, 2008, "Adjunct"

Quick Fiction, No. 14, Fall 2008, "Papel Picado"

RE:AL, Vol. 33 No. 1, Summer/Fall 2008, "House of the Ancients"

Right Hand Pointing, No. 21, June 2008, "No Sudden Moves"

r.kv.r.y quarterly, July 2012, "Year of the Rooster"

Six Little Things, No. 5, Winter 2007, "The Learned Lama"

Storyglossia, No. 21, July 2007, "The Pet Palace"

Contents

Part I: Nick & Alexis

HOUSE OF THE ANCIENTS

Nick—having learned from his Lonely Planet guide that the Mexico City subway is cheap, but infested with pickpockets—clutches his shoulder pack to his chest. He knows that the obvious anxiety marks him as an American or, at best, a Canadian, but right now, eyeing his fellow passengers, he doesn't care. He's been walking all day, like a zombie for the last hour. He's worn out. The blister on his heel burns. He detects, via the low-pitched growl at the bottom of his gut, that he might soon be laid low with whatever it is that keeps Alexis tethered to their hotel room. And now he needs to know—it's essential that he knows—that he is headed in the right direction. The guidebook falls open where he's dog-eared the subway map. He boarded at *Auditorio* and the train has just left *Constituyentes*. Good. South, just as he wants, toward *Barranca del Muerte*. Ravine of Death.

As the train pulls into *Tacubaya*, a sprawling station where three lines meet, he slips the guidebook back into the bag. At least the flood of new passengers won't identify him immediately. Unless the shiny Nikes give him away. Or his White Sox cap. Or his Levis and University of Chicago T-shirt.

When the doors hiss open, a family enters: a dark man with a guitar slung over his shoulder, a woman with a babe-in-arms, and two small boys. At the head of the subway car, the man unslings the guitar and hugs it close, plucking the strings tentatively as he sings in a piercing voice that rises above the train's clatter. The lyrics don't penetrate Nick's meager Spanish, but the other riders, who nod appreciatively with the staccato beat, seem to recognize the song. The wife takes a seat with the baby and keeps her eyes low. The boys— Nick has assigned them names, Roberto for the older, and Pablo for the little one—the boys make their way through the car, Roberto down the left side, Pablo down the right, each with a grimy hand extended, stopping before every promising passenger, waiting for a coin or a head shake, or a scowl.

It is tiny Pablo, wearing green sweat pants and a tobacco-brown sweater, who stands before Nick, gazing up at him with wide, dark eyes. The father's voice sails through the car, an arrow Nick thinks is meant for him, and Pablo bounces his open hand, a hand no larger than a cat's paw, on Nick's knee. When Nick presses a peso into Pablo's palm, there is no smile, no acknowledgment. The boy breaks his gaze and moves on. At *San Pedro de los Piños*, the boys jostle through the rushing passengers to join their parents, and the family passes into the next car, to be replaced by a grim-faced young man selling DVDs of a rock concert that he displays on a portable player held above his head, sour chords blaring from the machine's tiny speakers as the vendor maneuvers through the oblivious crowd.

The train hurtles through the tunnel, a passage in time for Nick, back to his Chicago commute, images of Alexis flickering on the black windows, their future together, healing the strain of faded newness, feeling their way toward something solid and lasting.

At *Barranca del Muerte*, the end of the line, Nick exits, passing through the darkened subterranean maze, up a series of clanking escalators, through a glittering turnstile, and into the harsh light of *Avenida Revolución*.

He fumbles for sunglasses, shades his eyes, and feels dizzy. His feet ache, as do his back and bones, the gut-rumbling worse now. His hands are swollen, and tingle to the tips of his fingers. The brief train ride has done little to salve the effect of his long morning's walk, from the *Zócalo* to *Alameda Central*, then to *Bosque de Chapultapec* along *Pasejo de la Reforma*. Was it three miles in all? Five? Whatever the distance, the sun did not seem so vicious as it is at *Barranca del Muerte*, bleaching the pavement bone-white beneath his feet.

It would have been foolish for Alexis to come, although she wanted to. She's not usually a brave patient. At home, in the Lakeview apartment they've shared for nearly a year, she expects to be pampered when she's sick. Chicken soup, foot massage, the works. But here in Mexico, on their relationship rescue mission, she said she wanted to power through. She'd take Imodium, she'd carry a roll of t.p., but she wasn't going to miss anything. Not the museums, not the pyramids, not the Virgin of Guadalupe, nothing. Calling in sick to a Loop ad job she hated for its crass superficiality was one thing. This was vacation. This was real. But when it came time to lace on her walking shoes, to leave the hotel room and tramp the streets, to be more than a few steps from the toilet, she changed her mind and urged Nick to head out on his own.

On the street now, the sizzle and smoke of frying onions bites Nick's nose and eyes. He hurries past a grill teaming with sausages as pink as bubble gum, startled by the thwack-thwack of a stooped woman pounding tortillas with her fist and slapping them onto a hot griddle. And then there are the boys, Roberto and Pablo, just ahead of him. The parents are nowhere in sight, but the smaller one turns and sees Nick. Nick is sure the boy remembers him, the coin in the subway, Nick the only passenger, certainly the only *gringo*, who'd come through. Of course he remembers. Nick's stomach grabs him from the inside and he believes he might vomit, or worse, but he clenches his bowels and follows the boys.

He's sure they're the same boys, there isn't a lick of doubt in his mind, but they seem older than he'd first thought, taller, less kid-like. They move fast through the crowd and Nick jogs to keep pace. They come to a thronged corner, with rushing traffic, horns blaring, like the noise the sun is now making in his head. One turns left and the other right. *Izquierda. Derecha*. He's lost them.

He spots a vendor selling Coke and it's as if this is what he's been walking toward all day. A cold Coke. Once he tastes it, lets the carbonation burn his dry throat, feels the bubbles rise insistently inside his nose, holds the icy bottle against his scorched forehead, he'll be all right. He can go on, start what he's finished.

"Coke," he says. "*Uno.*"

It's Roberto behind the counter, with Pablo at his side. He's sure of it. Roberto shakes his head, points to the label on the bottle. It isn't Coke, there's some other word on the bottle that Nick can't decipher, but the relief is the same. It doesn't matter that it isn't familiar, that it's a Mexican brand, because it will be the same. He holds out a five peso coin and it is Pablo who reaches for it with his filthy hand, now as large as a jaguar's paw. Nick looks into the boy's eyes, but there is no recognition.

He drinks. The soda is flat. Or not quite flat: there is some fizz to it but it's not what he expected. Not what he wanted. Not what he knows. But still he drinks. When the bottle is empty, he hands it to Roberto who winks at him while scratching the black stubble that has appeared on his chin.

Nick isn't far now from his destination—the studio of the incomparable muralist. With his thirst quenched and his goal in reach, he feels his shoulders soften, his stomach uncramp. He might splurge and take a taxi back to the hotel. He'll lie down next to Alexis and tell her about the museum and the subway and the little boys. He'll hold her, and she'll respond, and they'll both face tomorrow. A new day.

He turns right off of *Revolución* and heads up a steep hill into the heart of the *San Angel* neighborhood. The first person he sees is his father. A stooped man with thick white hair shuffles out of sight behind an imposing wall. Nick runs and the hill becomes even steeper. There is a metal gate, locked and thickly barred, like a prison, and behind the bars there is a sign: *Casa de los Ancianos.* His father is nowhere to be seen. His father has been dead since before the new century began.

Roberto is behind the gate, in the white coat of a nurse. He waves.

The studio is at the top of the hill, directly across the street from the San Angel Inn. Nick is wheezing when he reaches the entrance, he bends over, nauseated, hands on his knees, as sweat drips from his nose and explodes in wet, gray craters on the dusty sidewalk. His breath returns, he steps through the gate and is greeted by a grinning Pablo. Nick has his wallet out, ready to pay for his ticket, but he can't take his eyes from the gold rimming Pablo's teeth, the boy's thin moustache, the slight paunch that swells a too-small sweater. Pablo shakes his head, points to the sign that says *Domingo-Libre*, Sunday-Free, and with the open palm of his hand invites Nick to climb the stairs to the great man's studio.

It is a plain, square space, with a wall of glass providing light to every angle. In one corner of the room a book stands open on a desk, the painter's glasses marking the page as if he has just stepped out. Nick reaches for the book, he wants to see what the man was reading, but Roberto—it is Roberto with him now, Pablo has gone—shakes his head. In the opposite corner is an easel on which rests a canvas. It is a scene Nick recognizes, from one of the famous murals, perhaps a study for the work itself. He studies the crowd of faces gazing toward a mysterious glow at the edge of the frame. Pablo is there, his hair thinner, the paunch now substantial, leaning on his brother Roberto, hair gray-flecked, who kneels at the bier of Nick's father, shrouded in white robes, a single calla lily in his hand.

Nick runs down the stairs. He meant to buy a souvenir for Alexis, to share this moment with her, but he can't stay a second longer. He flees down the hill and feels his bowels surrender, filling him with the smell of his own decay. He comes to the House of the Ancients and as he passes its gates Roberto and Pablo, both frail and gray and withered, lift their bony hands in a tired wave.

IN THE PALACE OF CORTÉS

Nick is sitting outside at the Café Hidalgo, sipping his Corona, contemplating an upgrade to tequila, when Alexis finally arrives, breathless. He left her at the hotel, and he's been waiting. She begged to come with him, cried in big wheezing sobs that she didn't want to be alone, but he wouldn't hear of it unless she changed clothes. Now she's wearing the cream-colored blouse he laid out for her, the peach shorts. Not as comfortable, maybe, as the jeans and T-shirt, but better, more elegant, like a rich dessert.

It's a bright, warm day in Cuernavaca, probably zero at home in Chicago. He's wearing dark glasses. At the edge of the *Plaza de Armas*, just a hundred feet behind Alexis, is an enormous flowering tree, the likes of which Nick has never seen. It's yellow. Too yellow. It doesn't look real.

"There's some kind of festival," Alexis says. "The streets are impossible in this country." She's recovered from her tears, eyes clear, no makeup streaks. He suspects her resilience is inherited from her parents, farmers he's thus far avoided meeting.

Nick glares at her over his lowered sunglasses, in the silent way his own parents rebuked him when he was growing up on Long Island. Both psychologists, they never needed to yell. Not at him, not at each other, not even when they divorced.

Alexis turns away. She wanted to spend New Year's in Hawaii, or anywhere with a beach. He's always liked Maui, understood why it was her idea of paradise, but instead chose the rugged mountains of Mexico.

"I'm just saying," she mutters.

He does hear horns blaring in the distance, trumpets and taxis both, and admits the possibility that she's telling the truth about the traffic. The opposite is equally possible, but he's never known Alexis to lie. It takes a sharp mind to pull off a good lie. She still believes that he went to New York in November to run the marathon, and that he had a brother who killed himself in high school. He lies to her every week. For practice.

"What kind of tree is that?" Nick points with his chin, and Alexis turns to look.

"Yellow," she says. There's no irony in her voice. There couldn't be. Nor does she have the wit for sarcasm.

"That's what I thought," says Nick. "But I needed to hear it from you to be sure."

She sticks her tongue out at him. He's surprised by this. It's an ugly gesture, one that implies comprehension and courage, but Alexis turns it into a glamorous pose, so maybe not. She's a model. Thin, but not too thin. Long, lustrous hair. Nick runs an ad agency in Chicago and they met on a lingerie catalog shoot. He hired her for a newspaper spread, then a commercial, eventually becoming her de facto manager, deciding which jobs were good for her, which she should turn down. They've been living together for six months.

She orders tequila.

"Do you think you should?" he asks. It's partly concern for her weight. She's doing a swimsuit ad when they get back to Chicago.

"We're on vacation, Nicky. Lighten up!"

But the main reason he objects is that tequila is what he really wants but now can't have. He won't follow her lead. She might get the wrong idea.

Instead of tequila, he asks for another Corona and gazes again at the beautiful tree. He wonders if it's indigenous to Mexico, or if the Spaniards brought it. He can't recall anything comparable in Asia or Africa. He used a jacaranda background on a shoot in Thailand once, but those blossoms were lavender, pale and quiet. This yellow shouts.

Cuernavaca was also his choice. After he vetoed Hawaii and bought tickets for Mexico, Alexis studied the guidebook and said she wanted to see Oaxaca. Nick enjoyed an ancient ruin as much as anyone, and he wasn't particularly worried about getting in the middle of the local political squabbles he'd heard about. But how was she ever going to learn if she got what she wanted? He knew what was best. He made the decisions. There wasn't time for long bus rides or tramping around pyramids in Oaxaca, he explained. Their arguments even at home, like this one, were calm, often taking place in bed at the end of a busy day, and followed a pattern. She would protest meekly, he'd go on the offensive, and she'd surrender. Cuernavaca was closer, he decreed, there were museums and ruins both, on a clear day you could see the volcano, and that's where they would go. She opened her mouth to reply, and he, aroused by his own authority over her, closed it with a kiss.

"What's that building?" Alexis points at the colonial behemoth across the street from the café.

Nick thumbs to the Cuernavaca page he's dog-eared in his Lonely Planet guide and intones, "'Cortés' imposing medieval-style fortress stands opposite the southeast end of the *Plaza de Armas*. Construction of this two-storey stone fortress-style palace was accomplished between 1522 and 1532' and yadda, yadda." He closes the book. "Part fort, part palace, part museum." The palace is indeed imposing, with its stone parapet and corner turrets. The clock on the north tower has been stuck at 12:39 since Nick entered the café, perhaps since the revolution.

Alexis downs her tequila and, with a sidelong glance at Nick, stands. "Coming?"

Nick gazes at her and wonders what he has done to give her the impression that she has any say in the matter. She doesn't behave this way in Chicago. When they go out to eat, usually at a bistro he likes in Lakeview, she watches his eyes for the sign that he's ready to leave. He remains seated.

"To the fort," she says, waving at the Palacio, too impatiently for Nick's taste.

"Tell you what," Nick says, "I'm going to skip this one." Nick is already thinking of the argument they will have that evening in bed, how she'll bend to his will, and his arousal is almost painful.

Alexis should be panicked at the prospect of going off on her own. He expects her to sit, maybe order another drink. Instead, she glares at him, hands on hips—glaring is new behavior, too—before ripping out of the café.

Nick finishes his beer and orders the tequila he wanted all along. Although he is amused by her anger and the lovemaking it portends, the chafing Alexis has begun to display worries him. It's possible that he has gone too far. He could be a bit more flexible. He could, perhaps, allow her to choose her own clothes. It's a minor thing. She has fashion sense, after all. What harm would it do to give her this one freedom? Or maybe he should take the opposite tack. Rein her in further. Maybe confine her to the room for a day. In any case, he'll find a way to pacify her tonight and wonders how cheaply a truce can be bought. Just outside the café, under the yellow tree, is a pear-shaped woman with long, black braids, hawking garish placemats and baskets. Next to her, a boy grasps a bouquet of inflated Mylar balloons in various shapes, and Nick has his eye on the yellow happy face. It matches the tree.

He has a second tequila, a double, and Alexis still has not returned. He's in shadow now, the sun having crept behind the café, so the air around him is cooler. But inside he's warm. He imagines his body's core, like the bubbling center of the earth, and that makes him think of eruptions and that causes him to look to where the volcano, El Popo, should be. But he can't see it from here, because of the yellow tree and the Palacio, and he has to imagine it, a white wisp at the peak, smoke, or a cloud, he isn't sure. He stands, as if with the additional height he'll have a view of the mountain, and momentarily loses his balance. He laughs as he plops back into his chair. He rises again, this time with a grip on the table. Wouldn't it be funny, he thinks, if I'm gone when she gets back? She'll panic and I'll swoop in to save the day. Even better than telling her what to wear. He chuckles, glances around to see if anyone has heard, then enters the *Plaza de Armas* to find a good spot.

He chooses a bench facing the café and in sight of the Palacio so he's confident he won't miss Alexis. He pictures her coming to find him, dazed from the museum, and he almost feels sorry for the turmoil his prank will cause. All his life he has wanted this, a beautiful woman who is utterly dependent on him, who is lost without him. It's what holds families together. Lives that are too separate, like his parents', vested with too much independence, are empty. Those marriages fall apart, but he thinks he and Alexis might be ready to take their relationship to the next level.

Behind the bench, under the yellow tree, a conversation has grown heated. There are several voices, at least four, but he can't take his eyes off the café to count so he's not sure. He hears one woman, an older man whose voice is hoarse, thickened, Nick imagines, by cigarettes and *pulque*, and maybe two other men, both younger. Nick's Spanish is fractured, summoned from distant high school drills, and he is surprised that he understands snippets of what he hears. The woman, apparently, wants to stage a demonstration against the new mayor in their village, an hour's drive from Cuernavaca. "The election was stolen," the old man says. "A demonstration isn't enough." "But—" begins the woman. "Fuck demonstrations!" says one of the younger men. "*Viva la revolución!*" says the other.

The argument continues and Nick realizes he's taken his eyes off the café. What if she's already come back and he didn't see her? He's only playing a little joke, to show her how reliant on him she is. He doesn't really want to frighten her; he's not that cruel. For the first time he worries that he's gone too far. It's one thing for her to be upset with him, maybe without even realizing why. He knows that's the power he has over her and he knows how to channel her anger into pleasure for them both. But the anguish, the fear of losing him, of being on her own in this country she didn't want to visit in the first place, that's another kind of pain that he doesn't mean to inflict. It might even drive her away. That's what real pain does, and that's not what he wants at all. He feels a bit of panic of his own.

Hoping she's still in the museum, he runs across the street. Then he remembers his plan to buy the balloon and he runs back to the park, pays the kid fifteen pesos for a smiley face, and then back again to the Palacio. He pays another thirty pesos to enter and then realizes he won't find her. It's a big place, with displays spread over three floors and dozens of galleries, from the earliest days of the Spanish conquest and the conversion of the Indians, right up to a photography exhibit of poverty in present-day Cuernavaca. But there's chronology on his side, a logic to the installation, and he races time to catch up.

He hurries past suits of armor, mannequins in burnished silver, ornate swords and pistols. He barely notices bejeweled crucifixes and dark portraits of bearded priests. On the second floor balcony, he is stopped. Not by the security guard, who only raises her eyebrows when she sees the smiley face balloon, but by the mural covering the whole back wall of the building. He recognizes the work of Diego Rivera; its bright colors and crowded scenes speak to him, humanity captured in the anguished faces of his subjects. First, at one end, the conquistadors battle Indians and the jungle itself, and join with the church to enslave the people, who are driven deeper into poverty and despair. Nick can almost hear them weeping.

Now, though, he recognizes the voices of the villagers from the Plaza arguing still about the stolen election, and he is startled to see them in the painting, just at the point in Rivera's timeline when the revolution begins. The woman— she stands erect and noble, with a mane of black hair—shakes a fist at the old man. The two younger men, both draped with bandoliers, carry rifles. Fires burn in the hills, like so many stars in the night sky; smoke and the demoralizing scent of charred flesh settle over the plundered fields. Men dressed as jaguars rip meat from the bones of the Spanish soldiers. Nick is disoriented, uncertain of the way forward in time. There is shouting, shots fired, villagers running for their lives, and Nick crouches behind a scorched wall. Time stops. He is trembling, hot and cold at the same time. He smells death. He hears the sobs of old women. He tastes dust.

And now enters a man in white, a thick, black moustache splitting his face in two. Nick recognizes this man. He is Zapata, hero to the peasants. He carries a machete in one hand and leads a majestic white stallion. The *campesinos* follow him. The angry woman bows before him. The old man nods respectfully. The two younger men salute, their weapons clutched to their chests. A girl embraces Nick, pours wine for him. He drinks. The wine is bitter and rough. Shouts erupt from the village followed by an endless stream of men and women, barefoot children, and a menagerie of dogs and chickens and goats. *Viva Zapata! Viva la Revolución!*

More shots are fired from the crowd, celebratory now, punctuating the cheers. Nick joins the shouting, his fist in the air. *Viva Zapata!* And Nick realizes that the balloon, the yellow smiley face, has been punctured and hangs, deflated, at his side. He remembers now why he's come here and when he does, with his purpose firmly in mind, Alexis appears. She's grown taller, assured, her head high. Stroking the snout of Zapata's horse, she again glares at Nick, daring him to move, to command her. But he's surrounded. Villagers hold him at bay with pitchforks. Calm descends, the battle is over. He is lost.

Nick finds his way out of the Palacio. His head drones, like a hive of bees, and his teeth taste of salt and dirt. The museum is dark and he wonders how long he's been inside the mural. The guard at the exit, whose mustache reminds him of Zapata's, stares at him, blinking, and looks down at the lifeless balloon. If he speaks, Nick cannot hear.

Outside, the air carries the rumble of thunder. Or is it the volcano? Or drums? As he crosses the street, dodging traffic, the chill surrounds him like smoke and he can feel it in his pockets, up the sleeves and down the neck of his T-shirt, stuck to his skin like blood.

At the Café Hidalgo Alexis is sipping tequila. Nick sits. She won't look at him, and he wonders how to begin. He settles his hand onto hers. She pulls away.

Is this his fault? Has he done something wrong? The balloon, now completely flat, its smile dusty, lies at their feet.

He ties the balloon's string around her wrist. He tries to speak but there are no words. He was only trying to amuse her, to guide her. To bring her with him into the future. Was that such a terrible thing?

Alexis looks at him. He sees nothing in her eyes, no panic, no doubt. He is shivering in the cool night.

"It's cold," he says.

"Yes," she says. She offers him her glass.

Grateful, he inhales the smoky fumes of the tequila, sees the *agave* plants in the hot, arid countryside, defiant Mexican peasants battling for freedom and dignity.

He raises the glass to his lips. He drinks.

DOWNHILL

Since their trip to Mexico, Nick had been confused, and he was reasonably certain his condition had nothing to do with his increased intake of booze—tequila, bourbon, Scotch, whatever was on hand. The thing was, Alexis had ceased to be the obedient mannequin she'd been for all the time he'd known her, all the time she'd worked as a model for his advertising agency and then, in short order, moved in with him. Whereas once she had worn only the clothes he selected for her and ate only the meals he ordered for her, she had become disturbingly willful. Who had told her she could wear that sweater with those pants? Who said she could have the steak when he'd specifically told the waiter that Alexis, his *girlfriend*, he emphasized, would have the salmon? It was all so very disconcerting.

Something had come over her in Mexico, some sort of revolutionary zeal, and he didn't like it one bit. He longed to recover his dominion over her, to rein in that spark of independence before the flame grew entirely out of control.

But how?

"Let's go out for a nice dinner," he suggested as they were making plans for the weekend. "I want to try that new Korean and French fusion place in Lincoln Park." Fusion makes her crazy, he knew from experience. Last year she'd cried when he took her to the restaurant in Bucktown that served a blend of Ethiopian and Chinese cuisines. Nick didn't like the food that much—the combination made no sense to him, either—but it was nothing to cry over. Alexis just didn't understand the concept.

"Yes to dinner," she said, "no to fusion."

Now Nick was seriously concerned by this continued streak of rebellion. He knew it was the foundation of their relationship, this inability for Alexis to know her own mind. She had always been completely dependent on him. If she began to think for herself, what would become of them?

"No?" he asked.

"No," she answered firmly.

All right then. No fusion. He could understand her resistance. The blended flavors might not be to everyone's liking. A physical rather than a mental reaction. Maybe that's all it was.

"You're right," he said. "No fusion. How about—"

"Italian," she said. "There's a great new Italian place in River North."

He'd been going to suggest Italian, but now that she's come up with the same idea, he's reluctant. If he agreed now, what message would that send? But Italian was what he wanted. It was only a minor setback in the grand scheme of things.

"Took the words right out of my mouth," he said.

At the restaurant there was a wait, but they found a spot at the end of the boisterous bar. Alexis appeared bewildered by the drink menu the bartender handed her, which gave Nick hope that life might soon return to normal. As she struggled to make up her mind, Nick rolled his eyes conspiratorially, but the bartender, a tattooed hulk with curly blond locks, waited patiently for the order, his snowy smile never wavering. When she finally decided on a glass of chardonnay, the hulk promised he'd be right back. He was trained in customer service, Nick concluded, possibly ex-military. It wasn't nice to make fun of the airheads at the bar, no matter what the guy was thinking. Bad for business.

The bartender returned with Alexis's glass of wine and the Manhattan Nick had ordered and from time to time stopped back to see if they needed anything else. They ordered another round, no residual indecision on Alexis's part, and eventually the hostess seated them at a table in the dining room, which somehow was even noisier than the bar.

"The bartender was a dolt, don't you think?" he asked Alexis. Nick had concluded that the musclebound cretin must be even dumber than his girlfriend.

"I thought he was cute," Alexis said.

When the server appeared, Nick ordered appetizers—calamari and a roasted squash crostini—and a bottle of Barolo that was neither the least nor most expensive on the wine list. Would Alexis object? She'd already had two glasses of white wine, so might have wanted to stick with the chardonnay, or maybe she'd had enough. And did those appetizers suit her? Nick was pleased by her silence.

"What would you like for your main course?" he asked her.

"I've been dreaming of fettuccine Alfredo since we decided to come here."

He grimaced, and because she'd been looking at her menu at the time, he grimaced again when she raised her eyes.

"What?"

"Do you think that's wise?" Although she still had the figure of a supermodel, and spent hours in the gym to maintain it, she sometimes needed reminding of what she should avoid. "How about the cioppino? Or the salmon?" The illusion of choice.

"I suppose you're right, Nicky. You always know the right thing. What would I do without you?"

That was the meek Alexis he loved, bending to his will. Wait. Did he detect a hint of sarcasm?

"I was thinking," he said—they were lingering over their coffee, the remains of the meal having been cleared away, the Barolo finished—"that we're due for a fun trip."

Alexis's eyes sprang wide. She'd been fading as the evening wore on, but now looked alert.

"Oh, Nicky, that's a great idea! We could go to—"

"I was thinking Lombok, an Indonesian island. They say it's the new Bali."

Her face fell.

"In fact, I've taken the liberty of booking our flight and a room at a nice resort on the beach."

She looked positively glum.

"Is there a problem?"

"I don't want to go there, Nicky. I don't even know where 'there' is. Can't we go somewhere civilized?"

"Civilized? The resort is one of the finest hotels on the planet."

"I want to go to Hawaii. All my friends rave about it. Can't we just go to Maui?"

Before Mexico, she would never have opposed him like this. Although he'd known even then she wanted to go to Hawaii, that was precisely why he'd chosen Cuernavaca. The Mexican mountains were the opposite of the beaches of Hawaii. The lesson was, apparently, lost on her.

"We need to expand our horizons, Alex. We can learn something in Lombok, see another culture. What's in Maui?"

"Relaxation, Nicky. Beaches. Sunshine. Surf. Can't we just have a holiday?"

"I made reservations, my love."

"Unmake them." She grabbed her purse and stormed out of the dining room.

There were no Lombok reservations to unmake. That had been a ploy meant to gauge her mood, although it did sound like a fascinating place. He consoled himself that the trip to Hawaii would be much easier to undertake. Instead of interminable cramped flights, making connections in Tokyo, Jakarta, and Denpasar, they could fly directly to Honolulu, with just a short hop then to Kahului airport on Maui. There would be no risk of Bali belly, or whatever the Lombok equivalent was. And Hawaiians spoke English, more or less. So there was that. He warmed to the idea. He hadn't given in to her tantrum. He'd just changed his mind.

He had hoped for an upgrade to First Class. He flew often enough on this airline. Shouldn't he be rewarded for his business? When they checked in at O'Hare he asked the ticket agent, who smiled her insincere smile and told him ever so politely to inquire at the gate about an upgrade. He asked the agent in the airline's lounge and the answer was the same.

The gate agent was no help. "Sir, First Class has checked in full. I'm terribly sorry," she said.

"Are you sure?" he asked. "When we checked in, the ticket agent said we were first on the upgrade list."

"Nicky," Alexis said, "don't badger the woman." She tugged on his sleeve to pull him away.

He sulked in the long queue to board the flight.

Inside the cabin finally, they settled into their Economy Class row, with Alexis in the middle and Nick on the aisle. In the window seat sat a bearded man in a yellow flowered shirt, eyes closed, head slumped against the cabin wall. When the flight attendant reminded their seatmate to fasten his seatbelt, the man's belligerent reply made it clear that he was drunk, despite the early hour. And after takeoff, he loudly demanded to be served, ordering a double Bloody Mary and then fumbling with his wallet and credit cards to make payment. Nick assumed they served him just to shut him up.

At cruising altitude, with Alexis flipping through the pages of one of the fashion magazines she'd picked up in the airport, Nick opened the novel he'd brought from home, a thick one sure to last their week in the Islands. This isn't so bad, he thought. Alexis is happy. The resort he'd booked sounded posh. He might find someone to play golf with. And then there was Alexis's new bikini, which she'd modeled for him the night before. He felt himself harden uncomfortably at the thought. Oh, yes, this could be a very excellent vacation.

And then Alexis shrieked.

"Get your hands off me," she shouted.

It was the drunk by the window, sleep groping, or wide awake. Either way. Nick reached across Alexis and grabbed the guy's arm, wondering how hard he would have to twist to pull the thing off. The flight attendant appeared, then the male steward materialized, and everyone in Economy was looking their way.

"We'd like to be reseated," Alexis said. Tears had started to flow.

"I'm so sorry," said the flight attendant, "but the plane is completely full."

Nick stood. "We'll swap seats. Let the creep grope me, if he dares."

He stepped into the aisle, then Alexis followed, and Nick climbed in and dropped heavily into the middle seat, hoping to send a message to his neighbor. The groper held up his hands—surrender?—and shrank back against the window. When they were all settled again, the flight attendant disappeared into first class and returned with a bottle of wine and two glasses, which she presented to Alexis and Nick. Not that the incident was the airline's fault, but Nick had to admit the gesture was nice, and even Alexis appeared to be mollified. She rested her head on Nick's shoulder and clutched his arm. The creep kept his mouth shut. And Nick was grateful for the small victory. A little heroism might reap great rewards.

As the jet approached Kahului Airport, he reflected on what had brought them to Maui. Not only had Alexis made it clear that she wouldn't go to Indonesia with him, she had refused for days to speak to him. She'd shut herself into the guest room, emerging only to retrieve a blouse here, a dress there, from her closet in the master suite. She came and went without telling him where she was going. She neglected the laundry, forcing him to do it himself, perhaps the greatest insult of all. He'd contemplated the implications of her resistance. What would it take for him to persuade her to change her mind? She seemed particularly firm this time. If he continued to insist on the Indonesia trip, wasn't there a risk he would doom their relationship? But if he gave in to her wishes, wouldn't he be accomplishing the same thing? And so he slipped a note under the guest room door:

> *Dearest Alexis: I know you had your heart set on visiting Lombok—it does look like a beautiful place—but it just isn't feasible. So far away! And you know my stomach has been giving me trouble lately. I just don't think it's possible. So I'm afraid*

I must insist that we stick to my original plan of visiting Hawaii. I hope you understand. Love and kisses, Nicky.

He'd run out of the house then, afraid to see what her reaction might be. When he returned, she had emerged and was humming a pop tune while she attended to the laundry.

Now, on their final descent, despite the low clouds ringing the volcano, the landscape was enchanting. From the airport on the coast, Maui's jungle stretched inland, up the slopes of Haleakala, and the white-flecked waves relentlessly lapped the endless beaches. The landing was barely noticeable, the smoothest he'd ever experienced. They managed to flee the groper, who had also continued from Honolulu to Maui, and lose him in the deplaning crowd, Alexis sticking close to Nick at every step. Their luggage was already waiting when they got to baggage claim, and in moments they were in a limo heading along the coastal highway toward the Fairmont Kea Lani resort. Alexis held his hand and chattered happily about the beautiful beaches. Nick beamed. Order had been restored.

Rich coffee. Mounds of fresh pineapple. Buttery croissants. They ate breakfast on the lanai overlooking the resort's private beach.

"So, my love," he said, "what shall we do here in paradise?"

"Do we have to *do* anything? Can't we just lie in the sun?"

"Exactly what I had in mind," he said.

On the beach, Nick watched Alexis through the lens of his camera. Her new bikini was bright red, with a strapless top that looked as if it might at any moment slip and expose her luscious breasts. Click. The camera loved her. Click. She posed with her hands on her hips. Click. Pushing her hair up. Click. Now she trotted down to the water. Click. Splashed at the edge. Click. Wait. Who was that guy she was talking to? Click.

Nick lowered the camera. Alexis was laughing, the guy—a tanned, muscular life-guard type—was grinning an impossibly white smile. Sickening. But Nick wondered if they'd had enough of the beach. Couldn't they find something else to do?

"Who was that?" he asked Alexis when she returned from the water and settled on the beach towel next to him.

"Who was who?"

"The guy you were talking to?"

"I don't know. Some guy."

"What was his name?"

"I don't know, Nicky. Jim, I think."

"Jim. Of course."

"What's that supposed to mean?"

"He just looked like a Jim is all."

"Nicky, there was nothing to it. He's just some guy."

"Who was flirting with you."

"I guess."

"You guess."

"It was nothing!"

"Fine."

"Fine."

Later, they had drinks by the pool and a candle-lit dinner, and no more was said of Jim, although Nick kept an eye out for the intruder. Had they made plans to meet? Was she going to sneak out to see him? But how was he going to keep her away from the beach?

"I have a surprise for tomorrow," he said.

She lit up. Such a simple girl, who loved surprises. "Ooh, what is it?"

"If I told you, it wouldn't be a surprise, now would it?"

"Don't be a tease, Nicky."

"Just get a good night's sleep. Big day tomorrow."

The wake-up call he'd asked for came at 2:00 a.m.

"What time is it?" Alexis said groggily, pushing the sleep mask from her eyes.

"Time to get up, Alex. Time for our big adventure."

"It's the middle of the night!"

"Rise and shine, sleepy head. You're going to love this!"

They stood in the dark in front of the hotel, Alexis's head on his shoulder, her eyes closed. All the better, he thought. She won't see the sign on the van that advertised the tour he had booked to take them as far from the beach as possible. The van pulled up, already filled with other visitors, and they climbed in. Nick wrapped his arm around her, let her nestle into him, and off they went.

All was dark, but the van's headlights illuminated the winding road ahead of them. The other passengers snoozed, like Alexis, or murmured quietly in the dimness, but Nick watched, alert to the shadows and the excitement of what was to come. Alex would love this. Wouldn't she?

The van groaned as it twisted up the steep road to the summit of Haleakala. At last they arrived and those who had been sleeping roused themselves.

"Where are we?" Alexis asked.

"The volcano, my love," Nick said.

They followed their guide to the rim and gazed into the world's largest dormant volcano as the sun rose pink above the low clouds to a chorus of oohs and ahs. The guide—Nick now saw that he was a young man, tall, broad-shouldered, a neatly trimmed black beard that framed his firm jaw—was talking about the flora and fauna of Maui, many of which could be found thriving in the volcano's crater and nowhere else on earth. Alexis had perked up and was listening intently, a little too intently, to the handsome guide.

"And now for part two of our tour," said the guide, herding the group back into the van.

"Part two?" Alexis asked. Nick winked at her.

As the sun continued its rise, they started down the mountain. After just a few minutes, the van pulled off the road and again they all climbed out.

"What's going on, Nicky?"

"You'll see," he said. "You'll see!"

The guide began passing out yellow slickers, promising that the jackets would be handy as the group passed through the cloud layer and modeling how their helmets should be worn. Another guide opened a shed and began rolling out bicycles. They weren't normal bikes, though. When Nick got his, he saw that it had wide tires and no gears, but it did have heavy-duty brakes. The frame was scratched and dented, but it would definitely do the job.

The guide was explaining the drill to Alexis. The riders would start out together, heading down the mountain. There was only one road, so no chance anyone would get separated from the group, and near the bottom was a cafe where they would all meet for a champagne brunch to wrap up the tour. One guide would lead the way and the other would go last to mop up any stragglers, but gravity would keep them mostly clustered together.

"Haven't lost anyone yet!" said the guide cheerfully.

Alexis grabbed Nick's arm. "I don't want to do this. What the hell made you think this was a good idea?"

"Don't tell me you're afraid. Come on, it'll be fun, Alex. Piece of cake. Like the man said, it's all about gravity. Let's go!"

Despite his bravado, Nick was a little unsteady on the bike. It's not like he'd ridden much since he was a kid, couldn't remember, in fact, when he'd last been on two wheels. But it's just like riding a bike, right? He laughed out loud at his own joke as he picked up speed heading down the mountain following the first guide, an athletic young woman with long black hair that flowed behind her from under her helmet.

He immediately passed one of the other riders, a timid, older woman who was pumping the brakes, which was probably the right thing to do to control her speed but made for a jumpy motion that looked uncomfortable. It made him think of Alexis, though. He should have waited for her, at least long enough to make sure she got underway and didn't chicken out. Once she was moving there would be no stopping her. But had she even started? Or had she waited at the top with the macho guide? The road was steep and he was picking up speed, but he was also worried about Alexis, so he slammed on his brakes, skidding sideways to a stop. He'd wait.

One after another, the tour riders passed him. Now that he was standing still, some of them seemed to be moving dangerously fast. He recalled from the drive up that the road was full of twists and switchbacks, which would be hard to navigate at high speed, even for an experienced rider. He'd lost count, but he thought everyone, including the older woman, had passed now except for Alexis and the guide. He wondered if he should try to pedal up the mountain back to the starting point, but he didn't think the one-speed bike was built for that sort of climb. It was strictly a downhill racer.

Finally, he spotted them, Alexis and the guide, speeding down the mountain as if they were racing to the bottom.

"Nicky!" Alexis shrieked happily as she passed.

"Loser!" screamed the guide. No, surely that wasn't what he said, but it sure sounded like it to Nick.

It dawned on him that he was now the last rider of the group, the guide, who was supposed to lag behind to make sure everyone got down the mountain safely, having zoomed past in his pursuit of Alex. Nick pushed off and resumed his descent. He'd already lost sight of Alexis's yellow slicker, so was reluctant to use his brakes. As he picked up speed, he recalled the formula for acceleration of a falling object he'd learned in high school physics: thirty-two feet per second per second. That second "per second" was the tricky part, he remembered.

He rolled faster and faster, leaning into the first tight curve. He caught a glimpse of yellow disappearing around the next bend and knew there was no way to catch them unless he picked up his pace. He tried to pedal to go even faster, but without gears he was just spinning, completely at the mercy of gravity. He crouched in the saddle, hoping to at least reduce wind resistance and gain speed that way. The next turn was coming up. He should brake to take the turn at a slower speed, but he'd lose ground on them if he did, so he was determined to lean through the corner. He bent low over the handlebars, raised his knee, something he remembered from his youth, and felt the bike fly out from under him, sending him bouncing across the pavement into the brush on the opposite side of the road.

When he opened his eyes he saw that both he and the bike were on the edge of a precipice, saved from free fall by a tangle of growth he couldn't identify. Where was he? He'd been riding a bike, he remembered that much. It obviously wasn't Chicago. Mexico? He was in the mountains of Mexico with Alexis when she disappeared into some palace. Cuernavaca? Where was Alexis? And then he remembered. Hawaii, not Mexico. The volcano. The bike ride. The tour guide. The crash.

He lifted his head. He raised his left arm. His right arm. The yellow slicker he'd been wearing had disappeared, but when he turned his head he saw it clinging to the lava surface far below him on the slope. The helmet was gone, too. He sat up. So far so good. On closer inspection he saw that his hands were covered, palms and back, with road-rash scrapes that oozed blood. He got to his feet, but when he took a step, his knee crumpled and he fell, saving himself from tumbling further down the mountain by grabbing a spiky branch of whatever those bushes were. The pain—the thorns, his bleeding hands—caused him to let go, no longer caring if he plunged to his death. But he slid only another foot, and lay back, considering his predicament. Surely the guide—Jim, right? Or no, that was the muscular lifeguard on the beach—surely he would notice that one of his charges was missing and he'd circle back for him in the van. Wouldn't he?

Nick waited. He sat up. Now he saw the gash in his jeans that had exposed the knee, which looked even worse than his hands. He felt the ache there now, too, a growing sensation that spread to his entire body. Everything ached.

When after an agonizing wait the guide didn't return, Nick gingerly got to his feet without putting weight on his damaged knee. He hopped over to the bike and lifted it out of the brush and back onto the pavement. He found that the bike worked as well as a crutch and he could move forward by hopping and supporting himself on the frame, but he realized it would take him forever to get down the mountain that way. Why had there been no cars on this highway? Would no one stop to help him?

After progressing only a few yards, it occurred to him there was another way. Coasting down the mountain didn't involve pedaling, so he didn't need to put pressure on his knee. He could climb back onto the bike, push off with his good leg, and be on his way. And the brakes still worked, so he'd just have to work his way down carefully. Off he went, helmetless, jerking forward exactly like that old woman he'd passed at the beginning of the morning. He thought the guide would appear at any moment to retrieve him, and the longer that did not happen the angrier he got. He would sue the tour company for negligence. He'd sue the guide. Criminal negligence, that's what it was. Macho man would pay.

On he went, braking, coasting, braking, until the highway flattened and he finally came to the T intersection where he was supposed to rendezvous with the rest of the tour. The sun was now directly overhead and he had to shade his eyes to see the restaurant across the road. He dismounted—he could barely feel his leg now—and limped to the entrance. Dropping the bike, he hopped up three steps to the door, pulled it open, breathing heavily, and hopped inside. The place was deserted.

Where was everyone? He was sure this was the right restaurant, but the dining room was empty. She'd disappeared again, just as she had in Mexico.

Laughter. Alexis laughing. It came from the back, so he hopped further, discovering a private room in the back of the restaurant.

He stood at the door, peering in. The tables were littered with the detritus of brunch: egg-encrusted plates, empty pastry baskets, crumpled napkins, champagne bottles upended in ice buckets. At the far end of the room sat Alexis and the guide, huddling close, laughing heartily. The guide refilled their flutes and they raised their glasses in a toast that Nick could not hear, but there was more laughter.

Nick willed them to turn, to notice him in the doorway, but they remained preoccupied with each other. He was again transported to Mexico, the feeling that he was watching a movie. But, damn it, they needed to see him. They needed to pay attention to him! He took a step and, when the pain exploded in his damaged knee, fell forward. He cried out in agony and reached for the nearest chair, which crashed noisily to the floor along with him.

He closed his eyes, waiting for the pain to subside. When he opened them again, he was certain he was dead, as two angels hovered above him, and he was not unhappy to see them. But the pain had not left him, so perhaps he wasn't dead after all. Not angels, then. It was Alexis and the guide who stood over him, their heads haloed by the ceiling lights. They made such a handsome couple, Nick thought. He was so tired, and the pain was everywhere now. He let his eyes close again. He heard voices. Alexis? The guide? But the light was gone and he let the sound fade with it.

NICK HAS QUESTIONS

W hat's the worst that could happen? Will anyone even notice if I pack my bags, lock the door, and disappear?

How does one go about changing one's name, from, say, Nick, to, say, Jim?

Is it possible to make amends? Does anyone believe you when you apologize?

If a certain former girlfriend, who ruined your life, were to get married and invite you to the wedding, what is the appropriate gift?

Does suicide require courage? Or is it the ultimate cowardice?

What I mean is, how can I possibly go on? Do I just call an end to it, or do I find a way to survive?

Is Switzerland still a safe haven, or did that only work if you were trying to escape the Nazis?

Did Alexis outgrow me? Is that what happened? Or did I shrink in her eyes, which amounts to the same thing?

Let's say I acknowledge a certain amount of responsibility for what happened. Not that I did anything wrong, but let's say my efforts to make life better for us all were misunderstood. Do I still need to apologize?

If I were to apologize, not that I'm convinced I have anything to apologize for, not really, would an email suffice? A letter?

Or is something more personal called for?

If there were to be a new woman in my life, and if that woman resembled Alexis so much I sometimes call her by the wrong name, would that be weird?

What's the most obscure place I could go? Does it have to be in a foreign country? Or can I start over in, say, Arkansas?

What should I do with the pictures I took of Alexis in the red bikini on the beach in Maui? What about the ones of her flirting with the handsome lifeguard?

And the ones of her completely nude in our suite? The ones that exist only in my imagination, I swear, because who does that?

There's also the question about my future, isn't there? In too many ways to mention, Alexis was my meal ticket. She made the ads we created really sing. And now what? Where will I be without her?

Am I learning something about myself here? Have I reached an epiphany?

There were women before Alexis. Who's next?

Did I deserve my humiliation?

Will I ever see Alexis again?

Part II: Oliver's Travels

THE YEAR OF THE ROOSTER

Bali is the perfect place for Oliver. It feels like the end of the road, the end of the world, where everything stops. No pressure, no pretense. Just the waves on the beach, constant, tempting. The bars in Kuta, art in Ubud, temples, music, beer, beautiful Australians, men and women.

He's backpacking with a guy he'd met at the hostel in Bangkok, Barry, a sour kid from Brooklyn who couldn't wait to get out of Thailand and now can't wait to get out of Indonesia. He wants to leave, and Oliver wants to stay, maybe forever. So go ahead, Barry, go, have a nice life. Replacing Barry with a girl, or another guy, or both, could lead to a new world of possibilities for Oliver, arousing possibilities. But Barry backs off, says he isn't serious about leaving, and, to show there's no hard feelings, he's got a special treat for Oliver.

Oliver is skeptical. In Bangkok, Barry's idea of something special was a whorehouse. Not that Oliver didn't thoroughly enjoy himself, but that was Bangkok. Another planet.

Barry leads him to a café. It looks like all the other cafés, and bottles of Anker beer arrive, along with a menu.

"A very special menu," Barry says.

Special, indeed: blue meanie omelets, blue meanie soup (with carrots), blue meanies sautéed with onions and garlic.

They order the omelet, to share, and, when it comes, Oliver has to make a choice. This could be a colossal mistake. He's heard about the effects, that mushrooms are like LSD, which somehow never came his way during college, and, although he's curious, he's just plain scared. He wants adventure, he wants experience, but it could kill you, right? Warp your mind?

The omelet is greasy and gritty, barely edible, but that's hardly the point. When nothing happens, Oliver recalls the first time he smoked pot, how it had no effect. Barry is disappointed, too, and they go in search of a real meal.

As they walk down the sandy street, Barry jumps over the shadow of a palm tree. Oliver sees the same shadow, but suddenly it's writhing like a snake, and Oliver is rooted where he stands. Barry laughs and jumps back over the shadow, kicking sand onto Oliver's feet, and then he grabs Oliver, dragging him forward. When Oliver tries to pull free, they both tumble, laughing, into the sand.

As the mushrooms take hold, they return to their inn near the beach, where Oliver hopes to ride out the trip in safety. They sit on the porch, and he grips the railing, afraid he will fall or—and this seems a real possibility—drift into the endless sky. He's thirsty, thirstier than he has ever been in his life. A beer materializes at his side, and then it is pouring into his mouth, dribbling down his chest.

A rooster struts through the courtyard. It picks and pecks, cocky. Peck. Cock. Prick. Cocky cock. The rooster looks at him and speaks, but he's speaking Indonesian. Whatever he's saying, it's hilarious, and Oliver laughs. He can't stop. Barry pulls his dick out and pisses on the rooster, which is even funnier. The rooster cackles and leaps away. Barry runs after him, spraying piss on himself, on the rooster, all over. Oliver is laughing so hard he spills his beer, and that makes him laugh more. He falls backward onto the porch. His head lands on the hard wood with a thud.

Oliver opens his eyes. He remembers the rooster and he remembers hitting his head. He feels his head now and there is a bump. But he's no longer at the inn. He's on the beach. He's wearing shorts, but he's shirtless and barefoot. His skin burns. The sun is sinking, nearly gone.

He stands, dizzy. On the way to the inn he comes across a shop and asks for beer. His thirst is still epic. He reaches into his pocket, but his wallet is gone. He pats front and back,

back and front. He runs back to the beach, anticipating the relief he will feel when he finds the wallet. But the entire beach looks like someone slept there, sand troughs and sand waves, and although he does find a spot that seems right, there is no wallet.

Did he have it when they went for the omelet? It was Barry's treat, he knew he wouldn't need money, so maybe it's in the room? He runs now, with darkness deepening, and finds the inn.

The rooster still struts through the sand. Oliver jumps onto the porch. The door to their room is open, but Barry isn't there. Barry's backpack isn't there, either. Oliver's *is* there, though, open, disturbed. He pulls clothes from the pack, his guidebook, his journal, piling it all on the bed, until the pack is empty. His wallet is gone. The linen pouch with his passport is still there, but the travelers' cheques are not. His camera. The tiny ruby he bargained for in Bangkok. The batik he bought in Jogjakarta. Gone.

He slumps on the porch, as close to tears as he's been since childhood. If Barry appeared right now he might kill him. Oliver pounds his fist on the porch once—take that— and then again—take that—and again. The violence helps. He pounds the porch again. Better. He pounds the porch one more time and, when he looks up, sees that he's being watched. In the glow of a lamp across the courtyard, two travelers, tall and blond, a man and a woman, lift bottles of beer in greeting. The man reaches into the bag by his side, pulls out another bottle, and holds it toward Oliver.

Oliver rises. The dizziness—whether from the mushrooms, or the fall, or the sun—is still with him. As he crosses the courtyard, the rooster eyes him warily and then, in a moment of clarity, runs for his life.

IN HOAN KIEM LAKE

Oliver has just emerged from the Metropole's air-conditioned lobby and already Hanoi's damp envelops him. Beneath his shirt, sweat trickles. With a handkerchief he blots his forehead, but it's unstoppable.

Unstoppable, too, are the boys who accost him each time he leaves the hotel.

"Buy from me," they shout.

Postcards. Pirated copies of *The Sorrow of War*, *The Quiet American*. He once thought of them as entrepreneurs, but now he knows that the boss operates nearby, doling out inventory, collecting receipts. It's big business, Dickensian.

He waves the boys off and crosses the street, dodging cyclists and motorbikes. His negotiations with the Ministry finished for this trip, he can relax and reflect before flying home tomorrow. He passes behind the Post Office and joins the crowd strolling around Hoan Kiem Lake. The lake's appeal to the locals puzzles him. Litter mars its surface. Shore trees are stunted. A crumbling pagoda occupies a tiny, lifeless island. Each breeze carries the smell of sewage and decay.

More of the postcard brigade assail him and now there are boys with shoeshine kits. He points to his sneakers and shakes his head, but the boys are relentless.

The heat and damp are finally too much and he claims an empty bench. The black water ripples under a hot breeze. His eyes close. His mind drifts to a dark childhood lake, an unexplained accident.

When he opens his eyes he has company, a woman with a swaddled baby. As if on cue, the baby shrieks. He knows the trick: the woman's hand inside the blanket has pinched the child to draw sympathy and cash. He's not heartless, but there's nothing he can do for her, or for the boys who still hover. A *fistful* of cash will not help. He's seen it all, wherever he goes, the beggars and the whores and the boys. What the country needs, he alone cannot provide.

The woman shouts over the baby's cries. She holds out one hand while the other pinches again, screams renewed. He turns away, but she grabs his arm. She lifts the baby and swings it in the direction of the lake. She holds out her hand again, and when he doesn't move she points to the lake, swinging the baby over the water.

Oliver understands what she intends, knows the bluff. But he knows, too, that poverty here is beyond crushing. It obliterates. What if this woman isn't a con? What if she's come to the point where there is no choice: money, or they both die.

The woman shouts again and swings the baby in an arc that will land it in the lake, beyond reach. Oliver imagines the bundle taking on water, sinking, its cries silenced. In the water he sees the placid faces of the baby and his drowned brother. And in the instant before the woman might let go, he leaps, wraps his arms around her and the howling child, and the three of them sink to the hot, hard ground.

PAPEL PICADO

Consuelo's father shows Oliver how to place the *patrón* over the sheets of colored tissue paper and cut the shapes—angels and crosses in this pattern—with the hammer and chisel. They are in the workshop behind the family's cottage, itself some distance from the *hacienda* where Señor Ortiz is the caretaker, while Consuelo prepares *quesadillas* for their lunch. She has brought him from Mexico City to meet her family, a major step in their affair.

The aroma of garlic and grilled chicken makes it hard to concentrate on the *papel picado*, but Oliver tries to imitate the older man's technique. With each tap of the chisel his head pounds, and he is all too aware that Miguel, Consuelo's twin brother and the instigator of last night's tequila wars, is watching from the doorway, blocking the fierce noon light.

"Women's work," Miguel says in English so that his father won't understand. A sneer warps his lip.

"*Qué?*" asks Señor Ortiz.

Oliver looks up, marveling again at Miguel's resemblance to Consuelo, two impressions from one mold. Last night, in the *cantina*, Miguel caught Oliver staring. He couldn't help himself: Consuelo's lips; her brother's. That's when Miguel challenged him to a round of shots, and then another. Oliver had no choice.

Consuelo enters to call them to lunch. Oliver removes the template and lifts a delicate red tissue, lets the light dance through the gaps. He presents his handiwork and kisses Consuelo's mouth, his eyes searching for Miguel.

NO SUDDEN MOVES

I'm trekking with Jake, six days out of Phokara, nearing Annapurna Sanctuary. He tears up hillsides, skates down dusty slopes, devours suspicious rice and lentils like a ravenous bear. He *looks* like a bear, with his bushy, brown beard, his burly shoulders and chest. As I follow behind, always behind, I wonder when the bear will turn on me, engulf me.

We've come to a ravine, bottomless from the looks of it, lined with jagged rock. Jake scampers across the plank-and-rope bridge, turns and waits. The sun seems close here, at over ten thousand feet, and although the air is cool, the world glows too bright—the ice fields above, the terraced valley in the distance—and I squint at the treacherous planks.

"Come on, Oliver," Jake calls. Part challenge, part impatience. We've been friends a long time. He drops his pack, wipes the sweat from his dark brow.

I step onto the bridge, as boldly as I dare, but I'm thinking of Jake, of close quarters in the huts we've shared, occasionally a single bed, linked, always breathing his scent. He must know how hard it is for me.

"Ollie," he shouts. "Be careful!"

The span sways even as I take the first step. There's wind here, it roars in the crevasse, catches my pack like a sail. I creep forward, gripping the slick rope.

Just a few feet remain. Jake is within reach, hands outstretched, and it's all I can do to keep myself from jumping into his arms.

THE LEARNED LAMA

Snow fills the Ulaan Baatar morning. As arranged, Oliver meets Ganbat outside the hotel. The boy's ruddy face is soot-streaked, and Oliver knows he has slept underground, relying on steam pipes to survive another bitter night. Like many streetkids, Ganbat knows beggar English and has offered, for a thousand tögrög, to guide Oliver. Oliver's here on business, but wants to do the right thing, to help, so he'll employ Ganbat for one morning, and hope it is enough.

Oliver pays and they both enter the Choijin Lama Monastery. He thinks he sees disapproval on the gatekeeper's face, but he doesn't care. Ganbat leads him through the grounds, tries to explain the significance of the temples, but he has too few words.

Ganbat waits outside while Oliver browses in the monastery's giftshop, a jumble of handicrafts displayed in a traditional ger. He examines a Mongolian woodblock—Buddhist scripture, the clerk tells him—and his eyes settle on a row of tiny bronze statues. He lifts the smallest, no larger than a molar, surprised by its heft. The clerk holds a magnifying glass and indicates the features of the diminutive Learned Lama: pointed cap, raised hands, enigmatic smile. Oliver pays a small fortune for the statue and carries it in his closed fist, sharp edges biting into his flesh.

The snow is thick now, and wet. Ganbat waits for him at the gate, shivering. Oliver shows him the Lama. He presses the little statue into Ganbat's hand and watches the boy's eyes grow wide.

LOST IN TRANSLATION

No one knew where Svetlana was. Oliver asked Eduardo, the project manager, who only shook his head and pointed to the clutter of paper on his desk, as if that explained the absence of the office translator, the woman they'd hired from the Kazakhstan government employment agency. He asked Andy, Eduardo's assistant, a kid who looked more like he belonged on a skateboard in a New York City park than helping to run a multi-million dollar US AID project in Almaty. Andy offered the answer that had become his trademark: "NFC," which apparently in Andy's text-speak stood for "No Fucking Clue." Finally, Oliver asked Stefan, the securities expert from the New York Stock Exchange, the chief of party who was nominally in charge of the multivalent consulting assignment. Stefan had his phone to his ear and only shrugged.

Fine, Oliver thought. I'll grab my driver and I'll go to the meeting without her.

He'd been summoned by Professor Nurbayev, the head of the Kazakh legislative reform commission, to discuss changes to the company law that Oliver's group had been advocating, with zero progress, for months. The West insisted on these changes in order to bring post-Soviet Kazakhstan up to a regulatory level that would appease, if not quite satisfy, foreign investors. That Nurbayev was now at least willing to meet was, he hoped, the breakthrough Oliver had been waiting for. The two had, in fact, met briefly once before, at a reception given by the US Ambassador. Oliver remembered the old man as being cordial, disheveled, and shallow, a cigarette in one hand and a drink in the other, his eye on the golden-haired Svetlana. Still, everyone agreed that he was the key player on the legislative side, and if Oliver's attempts to reform corporate governance in this country were ever going to get off the ground, Nurbayev's support was crucial. So this meeting was more than just promising. It was vital to the success of his project.

He grabbed his briefcase and headed to the stairs of their Soviet-era office block, not far from the capitol. Where the hell was Svetlana, and how was he going to pull this off without her? Nurbayev spoke some English, having spent a year on a Fulbright at Harvard, but Oliver recalled that it was minimal-to-nonexistent. He had even struggled with the social niceties, the hellos and the how are yous, and Oliver wondered how he had accomplished anything during his time in Cambridge. Of course study was hardly the point back then. His grant would have been about fostering better relations between the superpowers, not actual scholarship. But if Nurbayev really did want to move forward with this reform, this would be only the first of a long series of meetings. Svetlana would be needed to interpret when they started the real work of drafting and negotiating. For now, he hoped, Oliver's elementary Russian and Nurbayev's half-forgotten English would be enough.

He exited the building, looking for his driver, Vladimir, whom everyone called Volodya. The project employed two drivers, both free-lancers with fancy German cars that Oliver assumed had been stolen in the West and driven to Central Asia like most of the foreign cars in the city. These were details Eduardo didn't want to know and certainly didn't want to have to report to Washington. He shook his head and held a finger to his lips whenever anyone asked about the origins of these cars or some of the office equipment that had mysteriously appeared without being authorized. The project didn't buy the cars, technically they belonged to the drivers, so their provenance didn't matter. For Eduardo, that was the end of the story.

Volodya and his pale-blue Mercedes were nowhere to be seen. He was supposed to be waiting out front at all times. He drove Oliver to meetings, drove him to lunch and sometimes dinner, drove him to and from the office from his apartment near the embassy, and that was it. Easiest job in the world, for which he was well paid, and all he had to do was wait. But he hadn't waited, and it wasn't the first time.

The other driver, Dimitri, was right where he was supposed to be, however, hovering over his black BMW, wiping away the dust that accumulated in seconds on the dry Almaty streets. Dimitri was Stefan's driver, but was also used by the other project staff members when necessary. And Oliver deemed it necessary now.

"Where's Volodya?" Oliver asked Dimitri. Both Volodya and Dimitri understood a little English, although conversations with the two men were always a struggle.

Dimitri shrugged and continued dusting his car.

"Off with Svetlana again, is he?" This had happened before and wasn't really Volodya's fault. It was Svetlana who had no doubt commanded the driver to take her wherever it was she thought she needed to go. Volodya was a good man. Svetlana, however, whose loyalties he had suspected from the beginning, was becoming a problem.

"I need to go to a meeting," Oliver said. He was never sure how much Dimitri understood and so he was careful to speak slowly and distinctly. Still, he got only a blank stare from Dimitri. "We go," Oliver tried.

Dimitri shook his head. "Mister Stefan," Dimitri said.

"No, it's okay," Oliver said. "Stefan's in the office. He's not going anywhere. I need you to take me to Professor Nurbayev's dacha outside the city."

Dimitri looked up at the office building, as if asking Stefan for permission.

"Look, I know you're supposed to wait for Stefan, but it won't be a problem. I'll tell him it was all my doing. I have an emergency. We need to go now."

Dimitri shook his head again. Oliver moved closer to him. He had no intention of getting physical with the guy, a much bigger man who had served in the Soviet Army and could no doubt level Oliver with one blow. He only wanted to make the point that he was the boss here, and Dimitri needed to do what he was told. But when he was standing next to the man, looking up into his bloodshot eyes, he understood the real problem. His breath smelled of the cheap Kazakh liquor the men drank. Dimitri wasn't waiting for Stefan after all. He was simply in no shape to get behind the wheel.

Oliver had no desire to drive on Kazakhstan's crazy roads with their crazy—and often inebriated—drivers, but what choice did he have?

"Give me the keys," he said. Dimitri complied. "Now get in."

Oliver had the address for Nurbayev's dacha, although addresses were almost meaningless in Almaty. He knew the general vicinity—a settlement just off the main highway to the west—and finding it would require Dimitri to ask the locals for a precise location. An important government official, Nurbayev's house would be known.

They sped through downtown. Traffic was light at this hour because private commercial activity, at least commercial activity of the legitimate kind, was still virtually nonexistent. Even so, pedestrians took their lives in their own hands when crossing the streets because a truck, or a bus, or an unmarked sedan belonging to the secret police, ignoring traffic signs and lights and speed limits, might appear at any moment.

Embassies and government buildings rushed by, then the one high-rise hotel and the one nightclub Oliver had visited. Before long the taller buildings diminished and the streets were lined with one-story structures, many of them empty, some hosting squatters, maybe farmers selling their meager production of cabbages and potatoes and cucumbers out of a concrete shell. Soon they were in the bucolic western district, where private estates—once the exclusive privilege of party officials but now available to any gangster who could accumulate sufficient capital—lurked unseen behind high hedges. To the north, vast wheat fields rolled toward the steppes. To the south lay the snowcapped Altai Mountains.

Finally they came to the turnoff Oliver was looking for, an unmarked road that meandered south toward the mountains. A few miles on this road and then it would be up to Dimitri, if he was able, to navigate the rest of the way. They passed a school that looked closed, an empty playground, a gray concrete building with a barbed wire fence that Oliver suspected was a prison, and a few modest homes. Oliver glanced at his watch and pressed on the accelerator as the road rose into the foothills. So much time had been wasted looking for Svetlana and Volodya, and so much was at stake.

He rounded a bend in the road knowing that soon they would need to stop to ask directions, when something leaped in front of the car. He slammed on the brakes and the tires screeched on the rough pavement, but the collision, unavoidable, was like hitting a wall. Dimitri flew forward, his head banging the windshield, before falling back and crumpling in his seat. Oliver waited for the car's rocking to stop, but didn't move. He took deep breaths, taking stock, assessing the damage. He'd been seat-belted in, and had hit nothing inside the car. He'd twisted his neck attempting to avoid whatever it was they'd hit, but otherwise he thought he was okay. He moved his fingers first, then his hands and arms. He lifted both feet. He looked over at Dimitri who appeared to be unconscious. Only then did Oliver open the car door and climb out.

Lying before the Mercedes, the smashed front end of which hissed and steamed, was an enormous goat, its neck contorted, blood trickling from its nostrils and ears. It was obviously dead and so, perhaps, was Dimitri. The meeting was lost, but now that was the least of Oliver's worries.

Racing down the hill to the right came a red-faced Kazakh, the goatherd, Oliver surmised, screaming and waving his hands, more goats following, bleating and nervous. But what could be done? It was an accident, and it wasn't his fault. The goat had jumped in front of the car and couldn't be avoided. But how was Oliver going to make this bumpkin understand? If Svetlana hadn't run off, if Volodya had waited for him, if Dimitri hadn't been drinking, if the goatherd had kept control of his goddamed goat, none of this would have happened.

The goatherd rushed at Oliver, brandishing his staff. He took a swing, but Oliver ducked.

"Hey, wait a minute," Oliver said.

The goatherd swung again. Oliver ducked again.

"Look, I'm sorry, I'll pay for the goat, okay?" Oliver took out his wallet and waved a twenty dollar bill at the man. The goatherd swung again and Oliver jumped away. "Forty, then?" He pulled out another bill.

The goatherd stopped. He wasn't looking at Oliver, though, and Oliver turned to see that Dimitri had emerged from the car. Blood covered his face and one arm dangled loosely at his side as he limped forward.

Dimitri shouted something in Russian at the goatherd. The goatherd shouted something in reply. Dimitri advanced, shouting. The goatherd, shouting, raised his staff, prepared to swing. Dimitri raised his good hand and shot the goatherd in the head.

The shot rang in Oliver's ears. He raised his hands to his head as he backed farther away. The two twenties fluttered to the ground. What had Dimitri just done? He'd killed the man over the stupid goat? How was that possible? Oliver was willing to pay, it didn't matter, oh, God, what had they done?

Dimitri retrieved the money that had fallen from Oliver's hand and stuffed it into his pocket. He climbed into the driver's side of the Mercedes, wincing as he maneuvered his injured shoulder, and started the engine. It whined and groaned, but it worked. Dimitri grunted something that Oliver didn't understand. Dimitri repeated himself, louder, insistent, and Oliver moved to the passenger side of the car, sliding into the blood-soaked seat.

Using just one arm, Dimitri reversed and drove back the way they'd come. But instead of turning east, toward the city, he went west, the engine complaining loudly, smoke rising from the tented hood. When they entered a village, nothing more than a few houses and a shop alongside the road, he pulled off, behind the shop, out of sight of any traffic that might pass. Dimitri went inside. Oliver followed him, anxious to escape the car, and listened to Dimitri on the telephone. When he hung up he barked something at the shopkeeper who produced a bottle of vodka and two glasses. Dimitri splashed vodka into both glasses and handed one to Oliver. Dimitri drank his in one go, then poured another. Oliver did the same.

In an hour or so, Volodya arrived in his BMW. He barely looked at Oliver but retrieved a towel from the trunk and laid it on the back seat, waited for Oliver to sit, and then put another one on the front seat for Dimitri. Dimitri gave Oliver's cash to the pacing shopkeeper, and then they drove off.

"We have to tell someone," Oliver said.

"No," Dimitri said. "We tell nobody."

"But they'll find out. The shopkeeper will say something."

"No," Dimitri said again.

Oliver imagined the dead farmer and his goat in the middle of the road. Someone would find them. It was a lawless country, but surely there would be an inquiry when a man was found with a bullet in his head. Questions would be asked. The Mercedes would be found then and traced. The police would come to the office and Oliver would have to explain what had happened. Oliver hadn't pulled the trigger, but it was all his fault. He'd been in such a hurry. The repercussions would be endless.

Or maybe not. The car? Stolen in Germany or France. Untraceable. The farmer, a casualty of the country's growing pains, maybe killed by a rival, another goatherd, for all anyone knew, a jealous lover, an angry boss, anyone. As for his own guilt, Oliver might have hit the goatherd with the car instead of the goat. An accident, unavoidable, completely forgivable. And maybe the goatherd won't even be missed? Perhaps there will be no inquiry after all?

"You paid the shopkeeper?" Oliver asked Dimitri.

"I paid."

"And he won't say anything?"

"No."

When they get back to the office, Oliver thought, he'd have Svetlana call Nurbayev. She'd tell him Oliver had gotten lost on the way to the dacha, had gone east instead of west.

"Talk to Eduardo about getting another car," Oliver said.

"Yes," Dimitri said.

A new meeting would be arranged. Excuses would be made. Svetlana would translate. The project would go on.

JUSTICE, INC.

In an abandoned factory on the outskirts of Almaty, Oliver follows his new interpreter through a dim labyrinth, down high-ceilinged corridors, left, then right. Her high heels tap and echo; his rubber soles squeak. Despite the extreme cold, the building reeks of piss and shit. Galina stops abruptly and knocks on an unmarked door that is half frosted glass. The glass is cracked, a straight, sharp line bisecting the window, and Oliver worries that Galina's pounding will send it crashing to their feet. The favor that he's come here to ask will be denied, his time wasted. But the glass doesn't fall, and, when a deep voice erupts inside, Galina opens the door.

As they enter, a thick man in a wrinkled gray suit rises from behind a desk, leaving a cigarette burning in a crowded ashtray, smoke curling toward the distant, grimy ceiling. The man greets Galina in Russian, and she steps aside as Oliver approaches for the introductions. Sergei Alexandrovich Petrov, meet Oliver Warner.

"Hello, hello," Petrov says, his accent thick and guttural. He grins, displays black-rimmed teeth, and vigorously shakes Oliver's hand. Although it's nearly as cold inside as out—the grey light of the Kazakh winter offers no warmth, even through the broad, tall windows—Oliver surrenders his down jacket to Petrov, who adds it to a fur-laden coat tree in the corner. Galina folds her red cloth coat over her arms and hugs it to her chest. Petrov directs them to sit. A white-smocked woman serves lukewarm tea.

◆ ◆ ◆

Almaty is the dreariest posting of Oliver's peripatetic career. Decrepit apartment blocks line dusty streets, the sky is perpetually overcast, and the people—perhaps understandably—seem to snarl when they speak. The Kazakhs don't trust each other or the Russians, much less foreign consultants, of which Oliver is one, and all the foreigners are angling for positions of influence with the government. He's come to the newly independent republic with an official U.S. delegation to advise the Justice Ministry on company law reform, which the country sorely needs as they transform moribund state-owned enterprises into publicly traded corporations. The Europeans, closer geographically, have the inside track on the same task. The World Bank hopes to outdo them both with two advisory teams. Oliver's not sure the Americans have a chance or if the locals even *want* help, and he's convinced that the only reason anyone cares what happens in this dull backwater is the mineral wealth on which Kazakhstan sits. It all comes down to money, and he has his part to play in claiming a share.

Oliver's assignment notwithstanding, the Minister of Justice won't meet with him. The President of the Central Bank is perpetually busy and finds new excuses to avoid him each time Galina is able to get him on the phone. As a result, Oliver has next to nothing to do—he spends his days reading back issues of the *International Herald Tribune*— and is in danger of losing his job.

It had occurred to him, however, that there's an alternative. He knows all about back doors from his years in developing countries. He's new to Central Asia, but doubts that it's much different from Indonesia or China, where connections are vital. He'd heard that the director of this new private law school—unique in the former Soviet Union—has had lengthy visits to the U.S., thanks to a cold-war era exchange program, and might be willing to help Oliver get in the game. It's Oliver's last hope, so here he is in a dilapidated warehouse, knocking on the back door.

He sips his sugary tea, and Petrov lights another cigarette. Oliver sees that Galina is on the verge of asking for one, although he's explained to her the risks for her unborn baby. Galina isn't married and won't discuss her pregnancy. After Oliver spurned her advances—he was in a relationship, he'd lied—she's said little at all. Like many of her countrymen, she's difficult to read.

"American?" asks Petrov.

"Yes," says Oliver. "Did you enjoy your time at Harvard?" Petrov looks at Galina, who translates. Oliver wonders how, with such limited English, he coped in Cambridge.

"Oh, yes," says Petrov, and elaborates in Russian. Galina summarizes: "Beautiful place. Many skyscrapers."

Almaty is not without tall buildings, although they're nothing like the Boston skyline. Oliver is always amazed at what visitors remember about America. The Chinese like the shopping. Koreans prefer nightclubs. Kazakhs—although Oliver reminds himself that Petrov is Russian and also an outsider in this country—apparently are impressed by imposing architecture.

More small talk follows: Kazakhstan's beautiful women, the neighborhood where Oliver has found an apartment, the rich variety of vodkas that Petrov invites Oliver to sample. And then, on to business: Oliver explains his consulting project and the difficulties he's had in getting the government's attention.

"I was hoping," he says, gambling that directness will be appreciated, "that you could help arrange a meeting with the right people."

Petrov nods and smokes. There is an exchange between Petrov and Galina that she doesn't translate even when Oliver asks what has been said. And then Petrov looks at Oliver through the smoky scrim.

"Our school is new," he says through Galina. "We have named it 'Pravda'—Russian for 'Truth' and also 'Justice.' You see that we exist in squalor, in this relic that may fall upon our heads at any moment." Petrov looks up. Oliver and Galina do, too. "There is much that we need."

"I see," says Oliver, certain that what Petrov is suggesting— what Oliver thinks he's suggesting—is, at best, unethical. Is his non-committal reply enough? Or should he flatly refuse to pay for Petrov's help?

"I could call the Deputy Minister," Petrov offers. "He was a classmate of mine. Perhaps he will cooperate." Petrov exhales a cloud that lingers above Oliver's head. "Or perhaps not."

"What, specifically," Oliver begins carefully, aiming for precision that will not be misinterpreted, either by Galina or Petrov, "do you need?"

Petrov needs better space, new books, and supplies, but what he *wants* immediately is the prestige that a foreign teacher would bring to the school.

It's a small price, one that Oliver agrees to consider.

When Oliver returns, Petrov introduces him to the students. Oliver feels their gazes following him to the front of the dank classroom, as if they are eager to learn from him. But he isn't a teacher. He's already formulating excuses as to why he can't do this—it's against U.S. government policy, which is probably true; it's siphoning time from his real duties, which, sadly, is *not* true; the students deserve better. For now, though, Oliver addresses the class.

He describes his experience, the countries in which he has worked, and his purpose in Almaty. As Galina translates his remarks, he studies faces: a plain blond girl in the front row whose cheeks are as ruddy as her bulky sweater; a stocky boy with straw-colored hair; a little fellow peering out of black-rimmed glasses who had taken notes as Oliver spoke and now, instead of listening to Galina's Russian, is watching Oliver. Oliver's roving gaze stops. In the center of the classroom is a boy with neat black hair and broad shoulders, stubble peppering his square chin. Out of place in this dismal city, he's as attractive as any model or actor and reminds Oliver of the temptation that ended his marriage. As he studies the boy's dark eyes, he becomes aware of silence in the classroom. Galina's voice has stopped. All the faces—the handsome boy, the other students, Galina—turn toward him expectantly. And, against his better judgment, he hears himself promise that he will return each Monday to teach about stock markets and corporate governance.

A week later, he stands before them explaining how private companies issue stock, how shares are traded, and how shareholders steer company management. This, he realizes, is the impetus behind America's involvement in stock markets throughout the former Soviet Union. Capitalism is desirable, and the markets will facilitate capital flows to deserving companies, but, more importantly, the introduction of American-style corporate governance will help democracy take root. Shareholders who learn that they control management are likely also to exercise their power over elected officials. When this hidden agenda first dawned on him, Oliver had resisted becoming a pawn in a geopolitical game. On reflection, though, he's decided simply to make the real-world message overt. "Democracy can succeed without Capitalism," he says when asked about his mission, "but Capitalism is corrupt without Democracy."

He uses this questionable aphorism with his students to introduce an exercise. Because he speaks only a few words of Russian, a lecture is nearly impossible. Teaching is not part of Oliver's job and therefore also not part of Galina's, even if her skills were up to the task of simultaneous translation. Instead, he proposes to get the point across through games. He has created an imaginary company and will issue shares to the students—the initial public offering for "Justice, Inc." The classroom will become a stock exchange in which the shares can be bought or sold, at prices determined by demand. Because shares carry voting rights, the shareholders will elect a Board of Directors who will name managers, and the managers must report earnings to shareholders. If the game doesn't collapse, if the students follow the rules, Oliver may establish a second company, thereby demonstrating the advantages and disadvantages of free-market competition.

First, the concepts must be explained. Oliver speaks briefly about securities and voting, and, while Galina translates, he again watches the students, trying to gauge their comprehension. One or two of them, including the nerdy kid he'd noticed on the first visit, have understood the English; they nod their confirmation as the Russian version unfolds. The dark boy, though, wears a mask of confusion as he strains to understand the colored pieces of paper.

When the class is over, Oliver isn't sure that anyone, even Galina, has grasped what he was trying to do with the mock share-trading, but the boy is lingering nearby and that makes it difficult to think of anything else. He wishes he had asked all the students to introduce themselves, a simple way to learn the boy's name without revealing his purpose. Perhaps next week Oliver can arrange for him to be elected to the Board, or named a manager. Manipulation happens easily enough in real life. Why not here? The boy is watching him, and Oliver wonders if he's noticed Oliver doing the same thing.

He approaches. "Thank you," he says. His voice is soft, tentative.

"You're welcome," Oliver says. "Your English is very good."

The boy blushes, shakes his head, and says, "Thank you" again.

Galina is waiting, but Oliver is stirred by the boy's proximity and can't miss the opportunity to speak with him. "What's your name?"

"Sascha," he says, looking down at his feet. "Short name for Alexander."

"Well, Alexander, it's nice to meet you," Oliver says, offering his hand. Sascha's grip is light, the flesh warm and damp. He's not a boy, really. A young man. Oliver is reluctant to let go. "Let me know if you ever have questions about the class."

Oliver wonders if Sascha would be interested in coming to work for him. Almaty is a poor city with few jobs, and he wouldn't have to pay much to bring the young man on staff, although in what capacity he isn't sure. An hour each week with him isn't enough. Oliver wants more.

After each session, Oliver stays behind, hoping Sascha will approach him again, but he never does. The young man nods and smiles as he enters the classroom, but always leaves with his friends when the hour is up. At the conclusion of the course, Petrov appears and presents Oliver with a small pewter vase, along with a much larger bottle of vodka, and the students all applaud.

"You will teach another class," Petrov says through Galina. It doesn't seem to be a request.

"I'm afraid I have other obligations," Oliver says, although he is tempted. How else will he see Sascha? But no. He must forget about Sascha, who can only cause him trouble. Besides, he has fulfilled his commitment to Petrov, and Petrov has not yet delivered on the promised meeting with the Deputy Minister. Oliver considers reporting Petrov's corrupt solicitation, but he realizes that he should have done that immediately, before he agreed to teach, before he met Sascha, and now it's too late.

Oliver sits in his frigid apartment on Prospekt Tulobaeva. The television is on—a Soviet-era film about the corrupt West, apparently—because the silence otherwise drives him mad, and, despite the early hour, to bed. He tries to read, but the flat is so cold that his hands tremble. He has purchased a space heater that keeps his feet warm, but little else, and has come to understand why the people in this climate drink heavily. In fact the vodka he received from Petrov stands on the table next to him. It tastes like dirty socks, but once in his gullet it warms him, at least momentarily.

There is a knock at the door. As none of his American colleagues are likely to visit unannounced, and he's made no local friends, this is unusual. There have been reports of robberies, even kidnappings, from the homes of foreign diplomats and consultants, so he knows to be cautious. He goes to the door, quietly so he can pretend not to be home if that would be useful, and looks through the peephole.

Sascha. Oliver has been dreaming of such an event, wishing for it, ever since he set eyes on him in the classroom. When he learned the young man's name, when they shook hands and he touched Sascha's moist palm, he allowed himself to imagine this moment, to conjure it, to make it nearly real, and so it truly isn't a surprise.

Sascha holds a bottle of wine in his hand, a cheap French red. "Gift," he says, proffering the bottle.

Oliver pours two glasses, and they sit and drink. He notices the backs of Sascha's hands, the hair on his fingers, the thick wrists.

"Do you have family?" Oliver asks. What else can he say?

The language barrier is too great. But the wine and Sascha's presence have warmed him. He finds it difficult to breathe.

"Good," says Sascha.

Oliver asks about school, hobbies, and friends, but every exchange is a struggle. Sascha strains to understand, to call forth one-word answers. They drink steadily as if to avoid speaking. Oliver finds crackers and cheese in the kitchen and that gives their mouths something else to do. When the wine is gone, Oliver pours Petrov's vodka.

Sascha's tongue is loosened by the alcohol. Speaking English makes him laugh, which makes Oliver laugh. He talks about classmates, politics, his girlfriends. He joins Oliver on the sofa, which makes them both laugh more. But Oliver knows it isn't funny. None of this is funny. He no longer feels the cold.

He touches Sascha's muscular shoulder, his neck, and slips a hand down his back. He should stop, he must stop, but Sascha, poor drunk Sascha, leans closer.

It is the young man's musky scent that makes Oliver twist away. He jumps to his feet. Sascha looks up at him with wide eyes, asking, waiting. Oliver stumbles to the bathroom, splashes icy water on his face. He pictures Sascha on the couch, the willing Sascha, and part of him—only part—hopes that the young man will be gone when he returns.

Sascha is not gone, but he is asleep, his head resting on the cushion, chest lightly rising and falling. Oliver sits opposite and watches, grateful for this chance to think. He could touch him. He wants to. Sascha would never know. No one would know. Oliver closes his eyes, imagines.

When he opens his eyes, light is streaming through the narrow windows facing the boulevard. Oliver isn't sure where he is at first, but then he remembers. His head pounds, his mouth is foul and dry, his arms and legs are stiff with cold. He is grateful that he doesn't feel any worse than that. He is grateful that he will soon be leaving this frozen, harsh country, although he has failed here and has nowhere to go. Most of all, he is grateful for the vacant couch.

Petrov summons him to the school. Oliver wends the halls to the office. He wonders what else Petrov will ask for, what more he can extract, and how they will communicate without Galina, who seems to have vanished. The answer this time must be no. Buying Petrov's aid is out of the question.

He knocks, enters, and finds Galina seated with Petrov, who smiles and smokes.

Petrov speaks, but instead of translating, Galina responds. There is a lengthy exchange.

"What did he say?" Oliver asks, too loudly, impatiently.

"I think you will help us," Galina says.

"Us?"

"Him."

"I'm sorry," Oliver says, "I've done all I can."

Petrov grins, and again he and Galina exchange words that she does not translate.

"What?" asks Oliver.

"He says 'you will serve justice.' The school, he means."

There's a knock, and the door creaks open. Sascha enters. He ignores Oliver and goes to Petrov, who embraces him.

"My son," says Petrov.

Now Sascha looks at Oliver. His smile is thin, his expression blank.

"But, of course, you know each other well," says Petrov via Galina.

Behind Petrov and Sascha, the gray sky has turned white. Snow dusts the tops of parked cars and the empty street. Oliver is even more aware now of the cold, but the new snow is inviting. It covers the grime of the ugly city, the crumbling rooftops. It's an illusion of purity, he knows, this blanket of ice, but it's all the sign he needs.

THE OPEN BOOK

The cottage Oliver has rented in Northern Thailand was once occupied, so they say, by Somerset Maugham. If the brochure is to be believed, Maugham wrote one of his novels here, although the absence of the book's name in the promotional materials leads Oliver to doubt the truth of the claim. Still, it's a fine selling point, a harmless exaggeration, and he's happy with the detail for his own purposes, explaining to clients and friends in Singapore where it is he's going for his getaway. Just a cottage in the jungle near Chiang Mai, he says. A cottage with a history.

He arrives on the connecting flight from Bangkok and settles in before dark, relishing the isolation: away from projects, away from deals, away from office intrigues. He might write something, take inspiration from Maugham. It's an ambition he's long harbored—more of a fantasy, really—but that's not the objective this week. He's here to relax, to read, to recharge.

Darkness falls quickly in the jungle, where it was none-too-bright to begin with. The daylight insect chirr is replaced with a more sinister din. Not just the incessant croaking of frogs, but shrieks in multiple octaves. Birds, maybe, at the high end, or monkeys. At the low, some species of jungle cat. Oliver checks the door, unlocks and locks it again, then pours Scotch from the bottle he picked up at Duty Free, reclines in a cracked leather chair that looks like Maugham himself might have favored it, and opens *Of Human Bondage*.

His sleep is deep, dreamless. In the morning, as the dim light returns, fresh pineapple and bananas await him on the verandah along with sweet tea. He listens to the jungle's voice change again and then, as his ears adjust and the adjacent village comes to life, disappear altogether. Bells chime from a nearby temple, although Oliver realizes that "bell" and "chime" are both wrong. It's more of a resonant gong that sounds and seems never to end, until eventually it, too, is no longer heard.

The temple is not hard to find as it is the center of village life and, besides, its golden roof towers above its neighbors. Oliver joins the throng on the grounds. He has not brought a camera, so feels no distractions. He will observe, memorize details, perhaps write about this temple, about a foreign visitor who, say, meets a monk. And as this thought occurs to him he catches sight of a young monk watching him. A novice, surely. He is young, a teenager, with a close-cropped shadow of black hair that frames his handsome face, wide brown eyes that distinguish it.

As the monk approaches, Oliver sees that he is taller than the others. His one-shouldered robe reveals a solid build, suggesting a life more active than contemplative. The monk bows toward Oliver as he walks, his hands pressed together in greeting.

The monk's crooked grin appears. Hello, he says. But it seems the limit of his English because he continues in Thai that Oliver does not understand. The monk points to himself and says Praja. Oliver says his own name and holds out a hand. Praja raises his and limply lets Oliver grasp it. Praja motions to a bench and they sit. But there is nothing they can say to each other, so there are smiles and gestures. Praja points to the temple and Oliver says it is very beautiful; Praja nods and responds and Oliver believes they are in agreement. The temple certainly is beautiful.

Praja is also beautiful, Oliver thinks. His chin is strong, with a trace of stubble. The ears are fine, the nose not as flat as some and when he notices this it occurs to him that perhaps Praja is not all Thai. There were American soldiers here, and where there are soldiers and prostitutes there are unwanted children of mixed race. Is that why he is here? Oliver wishes he could ask.

The gong sounds again and Praja rises. Oliver wants him to stay, even touches his arm, but Praja bows. Wait, Oliver says, and hands him a card from the cottage, the address in English and Thai.

In the late afternoon, Oliver is on the verandah of the cottage drinking a Singha beer and reading Maugham. He hears approaching footsteps and is mildly alarmed until he sees that it is Praja. The boy joins him on the porch and, to Oliver's surprise, accepts a beer. And now Oliver is presented with a choice. He has been thinking all day about Praja, about the strong boy beneath the robes, about the remoteness of this place. Who would know if he befriended this youth, if they shared more than wordless smiles? He looks at Praja's eyes, eyes Oliver believes are filled with longing. Why has he come here, if not for this?

Oliver stands. Praja stands. Oliver touches the monk's bare shoulder, feels the warmth of him, guides him inside the cottage. In the yellow electric light, Praja's skin glows. He stands before Oliver, waiting, and, when Oliver does not move, because Oliver is unable to move, Praja slips his robe over the other shoulder and pulls it to his waist. He is a beautiful man, hairless and lean and Oliver's eyes overflow. He cannot swallow. He can barely breathe. With this one act his life will change. This monk is his salvation. If only Oliver could move.

Baht, Praja says.

What?

Baht, he says again.

Oliver's trance is broken. His breath comes. He steps back. The boy wants money. This is how he lives. And now Oliver's choice is easy. He moves toward Praja and reaches for him.

He lifts the monk's robe over his shoulder, covers the boy's chest. He can't give him money, but he wants to give him something. On the table, by the door, there is the open book. He closes it, presses it into Praja's hands and lets his fingers taste the freedom they cannot know.

THE SCREAM

It's an experiment. That's all it is. What can it hurt? Oliver and Toni dated in grad school. He thought they were in love, but it didn't work out. There was another man in her life. She found a job, moved. They lost touch.

Until recently. He was newly divorced, posted to Bangkok, wallowing in the past, wondering where it all went wrong—with his wife, with Toni—so when the alumni directory came in the mail pouch, the weekly lifeline from headquarters, hers was the first name he looked up. A New York address, Fortune 500 job title, no spouse listed.

After midnight, after the second Scotch, he dialed the numbers for her office.

She took to the idea of meeting, stunned to hear from him (he thought, based on the long breathless silence with which their conversation began). He'd been thinking Paris, easy enough for both to arrange, not exactly halfway between them. But she must have realized that the lights of Paris, its romance, would be too bright, that his expectations would be too high, and she suggested Oslo instead. Or, more specifically, meeting in Copenhagen—another easy European transit hub—and taking the train north. She had a cousin, or a nephew, or uncle there—Oliver had been unable to follow her logic, and there was a side trip she was keen to take through a fjord.

So he flies to Copenhagen, Thai Airways non-stop. He tries to sleep. If she's in the hotel when he arrives he wants to be fresh. If she's not, he doesn't want sleep to tempt him.

There is no waiting. He arrives, then she arrives, by separate cabs from the airport. They must have touched down at the same time, and he wonders how he could have missed her. She looks just the same. She's thin—she still runs, she tells him when he asks—and her hair is the same lustrous brown. He sees a trace of gray, but far less then he's detected in his own thinning mane. Her glasses are gone. He wonders, for good? Or for show? They embrace. He's not sure if there is warmth, on his side or hers.

The hotel was her idea, a concept hotel, built into an ancient grain warehouse. The outside is unique, Oliver has to admit, but apart from high ceilings in the lobby, the interior is charmless, the rooms dark Scandinavian-modern.

There is just one bed in their room, a King, and upon entering with the bellboy they both stare at it, realizing that neither had considered the sleeping arrangements. But of course they *both* had considered the sleeping arrangements. The bellboy is showing them the bathroom, the mini-bar, the television, but Oliver is thinking of the bed. When the boy is gone, Toni throws her purse on the spread, as if, Oliver thinks, to claim her side of the expanse. She laughs, a nervous laugh that he remembers fondly.

Although they both say they are tired—her flight from New York is much shorter than his from Thailand, but it's a redeye—they find the coffee shop. The coffee is weak, the Danish pastry not at all what Oliver had expected. They catch up awkwardly. Her marriage was a mistake, she says, and thank God there were no children. Her ex is a Republican. Whatever made her think that could work? Oliver also thinks his marriage was a mistake, but he doesn't say that. He considers telling Toni that he's a widower, but he vaguely remembers mentioning the divorce on that first drunken phone call, or in the one after that to work out the details of the trip. She'll remember, anyway, that he's not a good liar. She'll see the signs. So he tells her about Margaret, about the constant travel that made their life together too difficult. He leaves a few things out—his affair; her desire for children—that were contributing factors.

They stroll through Copenhagen, examine the shops, eat lunch, and before long they are both dragging. They can't pretend anymore to be alert, and they return to the hotel. The bed isn't an issue. They're too tired. They sleep.

By the time they get to Oslo—the ferry crossing from Denmark and the train through Swedish countryside give them much to talk about—they are close to their old selves. He kisses her when they are on the train platform, they link arms as they wait for a taxi, they hold hands as they enter the antique-filled Bed & Breakfast where Toni has made reservations. They are undisturbed by the Queen bed in their room. The awkwardness is gone. *Now* there are expectations.

After a candlelight dinner of herb-crusted salmon and delicately steamed vegetables, a hot apple confection for dessert—the best meal in years, both say—they sip cognac on the porch. They swat absently at the mosquitoes, admire the late-night sun, and cuddle against the chilled air. They speculate about what it would be like farther north, what having no darkness at all would be like, endless days, and then what it would be like having no light at all. Their voices grow softer and lower, and soon Oliver rises, lets a hand fall gently to her shoulder, and she follows him to their room.

The sex is cautious, deferential. After, they lie together and drift into sleep. In the night, jet-lagged, Oliver wakes and realizes there is a gulf between them.

Breakfast the next morning is an elaborate buffet of smoked fish, cheese, dense brown bread. There seems little to say, as if they've exhausted their supply, and so Oliver is aware of other guests. There's a Japanese couple with two well-behaved children. He hears French and German, another language he can't identify, maybe Russian. No one is speaking English.

Apart from strolling around the city, which is far bigger then he'd realized, Toni has planned for them to visit the Edvard Munch Museum. Munch is Norway's most famous artist, but, as far as Oliver knows, *The Scream* is his only well-known painting. On their way to the building, a modern complex that is partly underground, Oliver envisions the iconic work, the open mouth, the hands to the side of a head. Inside, he discovers that it isn't a single painting, that

Munch did several paintings of the same screaming figure, that they are all more or less alike: the same head that seems to be melting, the same voiceless oval mouth, the same hands raised to the face in terror. What has evoked the scream, Oliver wonders. What terror has the figure seen? What would make Oliver react so? He pictures Hiroshima, the horror, the flames, the flesh melting. Vesuvius. The Holocaust.

Side by side, they stare at one of the paintings together.

"These are fascinating," she says.

Not the word he would have chosen. Disturbing, he thinks. Horrific. He says, "They're incredible." The Rape of Nanking. Tiananmen. Or something closer to home, more personal. An accident. A death. His brother's drowning.

Oliver isn't feeling well. His head buzzes, his throat rebels each time he tries to swallow. He forces himself to concentrate on the pictures, but they begin to move and he hears the screams, not just of the figure but of the hundreds, thousands who have seen the same thing, suffered the same terror. He's dizzy. The sight, the sound, are nauseous.

"I have to go back," he says. He doesn't look at her, doesn't explain. He leaves.

Now he's at the inn drinking tea in the lounge amid the jumble of antiques, gazing out at the too-bright afternoon. His head throbs. His body aches. She comes in and drops into the chair opposite.

"You left me stranded."

"I'm not feeling well." His voice sounds convincingly strained.

She shakes her head. "Not now," she says. "Back then. You took a job. You left. You didn't ask me what I wanted."

"You wanted no part of me. I didn't have to ask."

"I was pregnant."

"Impossible."

"Jesus. I can't believe you. What was impossible was us. How I ever thought we could make it work—back then or now—is beyond me."

"What are you talking about? What about that guy, that Jackson."

"There was no guy, Oliver. Jason—his name was Jason—was a friend. When you disappeared Jason helped. He's the one who took me. Stayed with me after."

"Took you? Where? After what?"

"Oliver." It's a dismissive tone. "You've always been obtuse."

"You had no right to do that." His head pounds and his own shrill voice is painful to hear. "You didn't tell me, you didn't talk to me. You had no right."

"Don't be absurd. It was a million years ago."

"What difference—"

"Stop it. Can't you see? I knew this would happen. A huge mistake." She turns and leaves him in the lounge, leaves the inn. She doesn't say where she's going. She doesn't look back.

He tries to speak but there is no sound. He knows his fever has worsened. His throat has closed and he imagines the swollen membranes, scarlet and coarse, constricting with every word. He can't swallow. He can barely breathe.

Part III: The Great Valley of Virginia

THE PET PALACE

Sandy knows she should tell Ash about the baby. And she will. Later. Not in the car on the way to their small-town jobs. Not when they've just quarreled about money she spent on a new outfit, a red satin cocktail dress she won't even fit into in a few weeks. Not when she hasn't decided whether to forgive him for his fling with that slut Ivy, who she thought was her friend. He claims he's broken it off, swore it with tears splashing down his cheeks like a little girl, and she believes him. She does. But does it make sense to bring a baby into a picture that's already so mixed up?

Ash pulls his squad car into the Sparksburg Pike strip mall and stops in front of Books Etc., where Sandy has been a cashier for six months, since the day she picked up her diploma from South River High School, packed two suitcases while her mother was having her hair done, and they eloped. Ash leans to kiss her, but she edges away. Is it him, or is it his limey cologne that turns her stomach? And has he somehow suddenly shrunk, his uniform baggy at the shoulders, bunched at the waist? He seemed so hot when they first hooked up, him a rookie cop, her a bored twelfth-grader desperate to tell her mother where she could put her nagging. Pull down that skirt! For God's sake put on a bra! Now the smooth, jutting chin she remembers has disappeared, the hard stomach gone soft. Is that even possible in such a short time? She thought his eyes were piercing, a steel blue, but now they just look weak and gray. Pools of water instead of sheets of ice. Was he even the same man?

The police radio crackles—a suspect's description, something about tattoos—and they both stare at the voice as if a picture of the man might appear. When the bulletin ends, Ash reaches for her hand. She doesn't want him to touch her, her stomach lurches at the thought, but she also feels guilty for her revulsion. On some level, she knows her mother would say, wagging a finger like the schoolteacher she is, isn't it her fault that Ash slept with Ivy? Isn't that what happens when you push a man away? Isn't that what happened with Sandy's own father?

To make amends, to offer the beginnings of a truce if not yet forgiveness, to buy herself time to think before she makes matters worse, she brushes imaginary lint from his shoulder. She pictures herself in the red dress—casually bearing the single red rose he's bought her, a night out at the only classy restaurant in town, the one with candles and a wine list, making Ash pay for what he's done—and she smiles. Ash smiles back, and Sandy climbs out of the car.

She's early, as usual, since Ash's shift in the Sheriff's office begins before hers in the bookstore. The manager won't unlock the doors for another hour, so she can't even kill time with her favorite magazines, the ones that transport her to faraway places, tropical resorts and European castles, with pictures of women in sparkling ball gowns and muscular men on sailboats. Real men. Not shrinking men who cheat on their wives and then bawl like a baby while begging forgiveness.

As she does every morning, she window-shops. At Kent's she spots pricey heels and a matching bag that will be perfect with her new dress. In the display at Kat's Cookery, a gleaming set of kitchen tools calls to her, although, despite her mother's efforts, she isn't sure she knows the difference between a spatula and a slotted spoon. A tiny pink snowsuit in the window of The Baby Shop takes her breath away. For a few minutes, she's forgotten. How could she forget? What kind of person forgets her own baby?

The next store, The Pet Palace, is already open. She had no pets growing up—her mother wouldn't allow it, too much of a mess—and, since Ash is allergic, she has none now, so she's always been drawn to this store. She hasn't planned to go in this morning, there'll surely be no pets now with a baby on the way, but as she strolls past, its automatic doors open invitingly.

The place smells of pee and damp fur, and her stomach rebels. She looks for a bathroom, just in case, but her eyes land on the big man at the cash register, attractive, if you like rough edges. Malik, Assistant Manager, his nametag says, and he welcomes her with a wink. About 6'4", shaved head, tattoos across both forearms and a blue snake creeping up his thick, coppery neck. Hang on. Wasn't that the description she heard in the patrol car? Dark, tattoos? Wanted for robbery, they said. Armed and dangerous. If he's running from the cops, what the hell is he doing here? And there was nothing on the radio about a strong, handsome nose or broad chest, not a word about brave brown eyes. It can't be the same guy.

She slips past the reptile cages, with their tongue-licking monitor lizards and sneering king snakes, into the dogfood aisle, and peers around the towering sacks of puppy chow to watch Malik at the register. His forearms are the size of Ash's biceps.

"Too much for crickets," says a white-haired woman clutching a shiny black handbag. "It's for my classroom animals."

"You want 'em or not, lady?"

It's something Sandy would say, fed up with her pathetic customers, but this Malik doesn't sound like much of a manager. Maybe the guy is here to rob the store and he has the *real* manager tied up in the back! She summons the radio description again. Did they mention the snake?

The aquarium next to the counter casts an iridescent glow over Malik. The shadow of a clownfish swims across his sprawling back. An eel lazes at the bottom of the mammoth tank. What if it *is* him? What if there's a reward?

Sandy flips open her cell phone and calls 911. "I think it's him," she whispers. "That robbery guy . . . No, I can't talk louder." She backs further down the aisle, out of sight. "At the petshop in the mall." An African gray parrot squawks when she bumps into its cage.

"Help you with something?" Malik appears behind her.

Sandy slips the phone into her purse and turns around. She looks up. A splash of black hair divides his bold chin, and the man seems to fill the whole aisle. She wonders if her baby will have Ash's mousy coloring and slight build.

"Just looking at the bird," Sandy says. "Beautiful. So . . . gray." Its beak is orange, the bird's only color, other than its beady green eyes. Not like any parrot she's ever seen.

"Nine hundred bucks," says Malik. He strums the cage. The bird squawks again.

"Oh," she says. "Guess I'll keep looking."

Heart thumping, Sandy rushes into the next aisle, a display of collars and leashes for every size dog, more varieties of kennels and crates than she can count. She peeks through the kennel bars at Malik, showing off for a pair of teen girls, letting a tarantula dance across his bulky shoulders. They remind Sandy of her and Ivy, not so long ago, skipping school, cruising the mall. Why has Ivy done this to her?

Malik cradles the spider in his hands and thrusts it at the girls. They shriek and flee outside. Malik laughs, a deep, lusty laugh, and drops the tarantula back into its glass coop.

For a moment, Sandy identifies with the spider. It exists in a glass house, no privacy, no life. Occasionally it's allowed to think its captivity has ended, that the mysterious walls are gone and it can go, finally, where instinct says it must. And then the hand, a force the spider cannot fathom, puts an end to the folly.

A distant siren replaces the girls' wails, and then stops— no reason to warn the bad guys that the cops are about to arrive, Ash explained once. She wants to stay and watch, her reward is at stake, but, on second thought, maybe it's time for her to leave. It's such a small town, there's a chance it will be Ash responding to her 911 call, and Ash is the last person she wants to see. She makes her way to the front of the store, keeping an eye on Malik. Slowly, slowly, she passes the hamsters (or are they gerbils?) spinning in their wheels, the guinea pig barricaded in its nest of wood shavings, the huddled white mice with their pink babies. The baby! She forgot again! What a terrible mother she'll be!

She moves faster toward the door and smiles in case Malik is watching. She's decided now that he isn't the robber after all, he's just a petshop manager with a fondness for tattoos, but it doesn't hurt to be careful. Then, before she can step on the rubber pad to open the automatic door, the cop car appears, its cherry top flashing, and screeches to a stop.

The store lights go out. Sandy turns and sees Malik's hand on a switch by the registers, his other beneath the counter. She steps on the pad but the doors don't open. Ash—she was afraid it would be Ash—and his partner, Kelvin, each with a hand on his gun, pound and push on the doors. She wants to tell them it's all a mistake, they've got the wrong guy, when Malik's hand clamps on her elbow, and he pulls her away from the glass.

She tries to tug free.

"I don't think so, girlie," says Malik, sounding like some B-movie villain, and wraps his thick arm around her neck. She feels bone braced against her throat. He waves a gun in his other hand.

Kelvin shouts. Ash opens the trunk of the squad car. Malik and Sandy stand by the cases of snakes and lizards and tortoises and spiders, and Malik stuffs the gun in the waist of his jeans. He flattens his hand against the glass and looks toward the cops. Sandy looks with him, tries again to pull away from Malik. Ash seems even smaller than before.

Malik pushes. The cases crash to the floor and shatter in a blizzard of glass. The snakes slither for cover, the lizards and spiders shuffle out of sight, the crickets bounce away like BBs. With one arm still around Sandy's neck, Malik flings open cage after cage and the store is filled with dozens of parrots and parakeets, banging against the windows and ceiling, screeching and squawking. All the dogs in the store bark, deep-throated shepherds in harmony with soprano terriers, as the big man sets them free. Puppies yelp. Cats hiss and arch their backs. Malik pulls out the gun.

In a second shower of glass, Ash shatters the door.

"Freeze," shouts Kelvin, his gun poised. "Let the girl go."

Sandy closes her eyes and wishes that it's all a dream— the baby, Ivy and Ash, Malik. She wants to wake up and still be in high school, living with her mother, and go to the prom and graduate and maybe go away to college. California would be nice. She wants to be anywhere but here. An explosion opens her eyes.

Malik has shot through the massive aquarium, sending more glass and fish and eels and thousands of gallons of water tumbling at the cops' feet as Kelvin clutches his chest and falls, taking Ash's legs out from under him, landing them both in the middle of the seething wave. Sandy screams. She forgets to struggle when Malik pulls her out the back door and shoves her inside an Impala low-rider. In a squeal of tires they rocket out of the alley and onto Sparksburg Pike, scattering traffic in both directions. Malik clamps one hot hand on Sandy's neck while he drives.

She worries about Kelvin and hopes—it's standard procedure, isn't it?—that he was wearing a vest. Ash said they always wore the vests. And Ash wasn't hit, was he? Wasn't there only one shot? She thinks she might be sick.

"They're not going to get me," says Malik in his bad movie voice. Sandy gasps for air.

"Baby," she says, but she isn't sure the word actually leaves her mouth.

Sirens chase them down the highway. Malik jams the accelerator and the Impala whines. She scratches at his arm but he squeezes her throat tighter and she stops. She feels his rough hands against her skin, wants to tell him about the baby, that he should be careful, surely he wouldn't want to hurt her baby. Malik steers in the middle of the road and goes even faster. Oncoming cars veer aside. The sirens fade. He's getting away. They aren't going to catch him.

He relaxes his grip on her throat, then lets go. He turns sharply off the highway, then turns again, heading into the mountains, pulls to the side of a dead, dirt road and stops.

"Get out," he says.

Ash is fine. Kelvin is probably fine. No need to worry about them. The wind swirls a cloud of dust in front of the car. She gazes beyond, at the hills and the distant ridgeline, and pictures Ash with Ivy, the two of them back in their small-town lives, shriveled miniatures of themselves.

Malik leans over her to open the door. He smells of sweat and animals.

"Get out," he says, louder.

"Do you like children, Malik?"

He laughs his lusty laugh. The snake tattoo on his neck seems to climb out of his T-shirt, out of the dark and damp of Malik's chest. He laughs again.

He's a strong man. He knows what he wants. She feels her belly. He'll be good for the baby, and for her, too. He won't try to own her. They'll be free. It won't be sunset cruises and champagne, no candle-lit dinners, but there will be adventure. There will be life. Sandy reaches for the door. Before she can pull it shut, Malik pushes her out of the car.

She rolls and tumbles and twists and finally stops, sprawled in the tall grass at the side of the road. The door slams and the Impala leaps away, dust belching up behind, trailing Malik's deep laugh.

She gazes up. In the clouds she sees a rabbit, a duck waddling across the sky, and a snake. She wonders where Malik is headed, whether there's someone waiting for him. She should have told him about the baby.

CYRUS AND JEANETTE

Way back, Rocky hired Jeannette to help out at the tavern, what with his spending long stretches in the VA hospital down in Richmond. She was a lot easier on the eyes than old Rocky, that's certain, even though she could stand to lose a few pounds, and her nose was crooked like it might have been broke when she was a kid.

A good listener, too. Rocky used to talk your ear off, fill you in on the comings and goings of our valley, flap his tongue on any subject that came to mind. But not Jeannette. She listened. She listened to Bobby Cabe moan about how hard life was, between his wife and his mama, the screaming babies, and the ghosts of all those war buddies who didn't make it home from 'Nam. She listened to George McKean gripe about the government—taxes too high, schools lousy and Godless, all the freedoms the founders intended worn to a dull nub. Hell, she even listened to me. "Travis, honey, how's Peg?" she used to say, and then she'd let me ramble on about my wife's latest treatments, back when we were hopeful we had the thing licked.

Jeannette had her own worries, too, including a no-good daddy and an ex-boyfriend who stormed into the bar from time to time threatening the customers if he thought they were getting fresh with his woman. Never mind that she'd given him the boot long ago; Cyrus had staked his claim. She never let any of that get to her, though. Unruffled. Quiet.

"I can handle your ex," said Bobby one night when Jeannette let him put his arms around her by the jukebox.

For the umpteenth time that evening we were listening to the Statlers croon "Flowers on the Wall." That was one of Peg's favorites, too.

"You be careful," said Jeannette, but she didn't remove herself from Bobby's arms. It was a rare moment of weakness. Made me notice her pretty green eyes.

"He's just another grunt," said Bobby. "Speak the same language, Cyrus and me."

"You don't know him like I do, Bobby. Cyrus is crazy. He thinks I'll take his stinking-self back if he manages to scare off every man in the county, and he means to try."

It wasn't long after that when a bruise blossomed on Jeannette's cheek, in the irregular shape of our state, and I knew she had let the son of a bitch come home. I almost wanted to shake her myself, tell her she didn't have to settle for the likes of Cyrus.

"Anything I can do?" I asked.

"I'm fine, Travis," she said. "Nothing I can't handle."

Late one quiet Tuesday night, I sat in my spot in the corner booth nursing a beer. A couple of regulars were in the back room shooting pool. Now and then the balls clicked and there was the satisfying thump of a shot finding the pocket, followed by laughter or a good-natured curse. I watched Jeannette out of the corner of my eye while she went about her business, pouring drinks, washing glasses. Like always, George and Bobby occupied opposite ends of the bar.

The tavern door banged open against the jukebox, sending the needle screeching across "Bed of Roses," another of Peg's favorites. Cyrus stood there in the open door, the eerie red light of the Bud sign in the window flashing behind him.

"Cy, what the hell are you doing?" Jeannette had just lit a cigarette and smoke streamed out of her nostrils like fire from a dragon. Bobby and George both looked up from their Buds.

"You're coming home with me. Now."

"You know I can't do that. Rocky counts on me. I'll be home when I get there. Same as always."

I didn't think her talk would have been so brave if she weren't standing behind that big bar that Rocky built himself. Like a fort it was, and Cyrus would have had to make some serious moves to get her, not so easy since he flipped his Harley a couple winters back, banged up a knee and a shoulder in the process.

Cyrus glared at us all, his face red, practically steaming, but he spun around and banged back out the door.

When he was gone, I sidled up to the bar for a fresh one. In the old days, when my Peg was still with us and waiting at home, I'd stop in Rocky's for a quick snort, shoot the breeze after having my head buried all day in engine guts, sucking grease and fumes into my lungs. Just a whiff of Jeannette, cherries most nights, was enough to lift me up, to help me face the sickroom our little house had become. But with Peg gone I was in no hurry, and I thought, for a change, after her man's latest outburst, Jeannette might be in the mood to talk.

"Why do you put up with Cyrus?" I asked.

"He's not a bad sort, you know."

"No?"

"Could be worse."

"You mean like us?" I nodded to Bobby and George.

"You know who I mean."

I nodded and gulped my beer. She was talking about her father, a drunk who, as far as we knew, was still rotting in jail for what he did to her mother. Strange that it was me doing the listening.

"Could be way worse."

"Cy's always been trouble, J."

"He just gets angry sometimes. Don't we all?"

"There's anger, and then there's anger."

The truth was, Cyrus's temper was just about the only thing Jeannette found fault with in her man, and she came out with the whole story, as if it was something I hadn't always known. We all went to school together, even Bobby and George, so it's hard to imagine any of us had secrets. It was all over school when Jeannette's daddy shot her mother in the head, and from then on she lived with her grandmother, who was half blind and all deaf. Cyrus, tackle on the championship South River High School football team, had let her pretend she was a virgin the first time they did it, on the couch in her grandmother's damp basement. We all knew what they were up to, just like we knew who had a chance of making it in the world and who didn't. She got mad at him when he joined the Army after graduation without talking to her first, and so she didn't say no when Dwight—that was Rocky's part-time bartender back then—asked her home with him one night after closing. And with Cyrus thousands of miles west, those two might have gotten married anyway, even if Jeannette hadn't lied to Dwight about her IUD and wound up pregnant. She lost the baby after the wedding, right about the time Cyrus got himself shot in Vietnam and came home. Wounded and ornery, but upright and breathing fire. Dwight didn't stay in the picture too long after that, and she and Cyrus had been together, off and on, ever since.

Like I said, no secrets, but it was nice to hear her tell it, the good times, too, the football games and dances, her voice warm and raspy, and both of us all smiles remembering the old days.

There was another night that Cyrus stormed in, a winter night with wind howling and snow pelting the big window like it wanted to come inside where it was warm. We were all in our places, watching him stride toward the bar, not bothering to shake the snow out of his wild long hair, letting it melt and run down his leathery face like tears.

Jeannette stepped back, despite the bar between them.

"Now, Cy, just go on home," she said.

"I don't like you being here with these three. Don't trust 'em."

We all stared at him.

Jeannette laughed. "They're old friends, Cy. And customers. I work here, remember?"

Cyrus wasn't dumb. On one of her rare talkative days Jeannette said he read the newspaper every morning, borrowed a book from the library from time to time. He could have gone to college if Vietnam hadn't taken him away. But sometimes he just didn't make any sense, especially when it came to her. Not that I blamed him.

Cyrus was breathing heavy, like he was getting ready to explode. The snow dripped off him and plunked on the floor. Bobby let his eyes drift back to his beer, but George climbed down from his stool and moved toward Cyrus as if he meant to tell him off. George was a carpenter, built fancy cabinets for the new houses going in up by the reservoir, and he could probably hold his own, even plastered, against, say, Bobby, who never recovered from the war, or me, who didn't play in but one football game in school because I was too skinny and too short. But George was no match for Cyrus, who outweighed him by about fifty pounds, had nearly a foot on him, and made his living, if you could call it that, laying asphalt for Red's Paving, lifting and shoveling and hauling all day every day.

As George took a step toward him, I held tight to my beer. Cyrus seemed to swell even bigger, reached over George, grabbed the back of his shirt with both hands, and flung him across the tavern like a sack of garbage. There was a thud when George's head hit the post in the middle of the room, sending thumbtacked coasters and business cards flying, and George himself crumpled to the floor.

"Jesus, Cy, what have you done now?" Jeannette slipped under the counter at the end of the bar and ran to George, whose eyes were open and blinking as he stumbled to get to his feet.

Bobby stood up then, looking for all the world like he intended to offer himself up as the next victim, but, instead, he edged along the wall, keeping Cyrus in his sights, and hurried out the back door. If Cyrus was looking at me, waiting for me to make a move, I couldn't tell you. Right about then I found the label on my bottle of beer to be mighty fine reading.

After that, Cyrus didn't come around. Days passed at Rocky's with Bobby and George and me in our spots, Jeannette behind the bar. George sported a bandage across his forehead for a while, and winced at sudden noises. We had one of the biggest snowstorms I can remember, must have dumped two feet of snow on us, and still we were all there. Bobby's wife left him, took their kids with her, and his head hung lower than the teats on a milk cow for a while. He moaned about missing his boy, wanting his little girl. George talked up the idea of a tax revolt, said if nobody paid taxes they'd have to leave us all alone, which made some sense to me, except I didn't pay a lot of taxes anyway, hadn't noticed anyone interfering in my business up to then, and didn't see how any of it would make much difference. I reminisced about Peg. Jeannette listened and smoked and nodded.

At home, I opened the windows. I liked how the cold breeze moved inside, pushed all the old, dead air out.

One dark afternoon toward the end of winter as I was closing up the shop, I saw the grease on my hands, the black mess under my nails. I tried to rub it off with a shop rag, but that just moved it around from one finger to the next. In the bathroom I found some sweet-smelling goop that was supposed to cut through that grease, and I covered my hands with it, half way up my arms. That seemed to make a dent, so I rinsed off and started over.

When I got to Rocky's, Jeannette was at the jukebox and a new tune was playing, one I didn't know, another Statlers number it sounded like, with fine harmony. Peg would have liked it. I made it to my booth, humming along with the new song, and was ready to slide in when I took a u-turn and sat myself at the center of the bar. Bobby raised his eyebrows, and George scratched the scar on this forehead. Even Jeannette had her eyes narrowed, kept them on me as she came back behind the bar and set a cold Bud on a coaster in front of me.

"You feeling okay, Travis?"

"Thought a change of scenery'd be nice."

"You're not wrong," she said. For the first time in a while there was a smile on her face. "You're not wrong."

It wasn't long after that Jeannette cut her hair—instead of being pouffy, like it always used to be, it looked like a basket of curls, with little silver streaks everywhere. I thought I could use a change, too. I'd always had a scruffy beard, even when Peg was alive, and I shaved that off. My face itched like the devil but I was glad to be rid of the thing. Made me feel lighter. Younger.

Jeannette showed up at the bar one night in a dress, blue with yellow flowers of some kind. She still smelled of cherries. She didn't talk any more than normal, but her smile seemed wider.

Spring teased us for a couple of weeks. We'd have a warm spell, then ice, the redbuds blossomed and there was snow, and then the air was warm and damp and smelled of earth, and you could just tell it was there to stay. No turning back.

One afternoon I noticed it was still light when I closed up the shop. I scrubbed my hands like I'd been doing lately, till they were pink and raw. I pulled off my coveralls and put on a shirt with a collar that I'd brought from home. It wasn't new. It was one Peg bought for me years ago, but I hadn't worn it much so it looked nice. My stomach churned as I walked down the street to Rocky's and I rehearsed what I planned to say. Small steps. A new beginning for everybody. A flower shop caught my eye and I saw something better than words.

Stepping inside the tavern, I whipped the bouquet of pale daffodils behind my back so Bobby and George wouldn't see. Jeannette stood behind the bar with Rocky who hadn't been around much. It seemed like she was dancing to "Flowers on the Wall" and she was definitely singing along. She looked up and waved. It was a shy little wave, which I took as a good sign.

Until I realized there was someone right behind me.

"What're the flowers for, Travis?" Cyrus looked down at me. His freshly shaved face shone, his hair was pulled back in a ponytail and there was a bolo-tie around his neck. "Got you a girl?"

Now Jeannette was beside us, handing me a beer, bouncing on her toes, and I saw sprigs of flowers in her hair, those little white ones that look like snow. She wore another new dress, off white, like cream, and she was grinning wide. Cyrus took her arm. The daffodils in my hand felt heavy and cold and dead.

"Those for me?" Jeannette reached behind me for the flowers and pried them gently from my fingers. "They're beautiful, Travis. You going to wish us luck?" She leaned close to me and kissed my cheek.

She waved at Bobby and George and sickly Rocky behind the bar. Cyrus held the door open, letting in the warm scent of rain. A car splashed by and I could hear it fade down the street, toward the edge of town, where it would keep on going, out past the house I'd shared with Peg, the moon shining down on it like the hand of God.

For a moment I wanted to be there with her, to relive the good days, before she got sick, to sit on our porch in the moonlight like it would last forever. But only for a moment.

As Jeannette passed out the door with Cyrus, the light was gone. I looked at the beer in my hand, at all the ones that preceded it. They were only a dim memory now, a fading glimpse of Peg, of our hard past together in this Valley, like the washed-out colors in a snapshot of your childhood, like the vivid dream you were sure would be with you forever but with the light of morning evaporates into nothing.

LAST CALL

It's last call for the Class of 2001, their five-year reunion drawing to a close, and Brenner, in his standard T-shirt and holey jeans, has just arrived. Dora won't be there, but he's come all the same. Elbowing his way to the bar, he bumps big Sean's arm. Beer sloshes on the ex-fullback's boots.

Sean glares at him. Brenner remembers Sean—a bully who headed into the Marines after graduation—but there's no sign Sean remembers him. Why would he? Sean's folks have a big-ass house across from the football field. School wasn't Brenner's thing, all that rah-rah bullshit. He's the same cipher he always was, runt offspring of no-account parents.

Brenner downs a whiskey, mutters, "Sorry," and reaches for his beer. Sean's sledgehammer hand pins Brenner's wrist to the bar.

"I said I was sorry, Chuckles," says Brenner.

The heel of Sean's other hand blasts Brenner's chin, and he crumples to the tavern floor. Sean brushes his palms on his camouflage jacket, and pushes outside. Brenner peers at the faces spinning above him. One comes close, someone familiar, a guy he used to know, arms reaching out, pulling him up.

"Jesus, what was that about?" asks Jason.

Brenner has heard that Jason is home for the summer, having dropped out of college for the third time. They used to hang out some, get high, in the old days.

Brenner turns, jaw on fire, sees no sign of the bigger man. "Sean's still an asshole," he says. "Iraq didn't change shit."

Nothing's the way it was supposed to be. Brenner has a kid he rarely sees. Dora wouldn't marry him, and the only thing they talk about now is child support. Jason says his folks split up and his dad moved in with some girl who's barely out of high school.

Jason grabs a twelve-pack at the 7-Eleven on Frontier Drive. They pull to the side of a dark road and sit in Brenner's pickup, drinking and smoking a joint, reliving old times. Brenner wishes he had a picture of the kid to show Jason. He rubs his wrist. It's bad news. He works construction when he can, plays bass in a Ramones cover band; even if his wrist isn't broken it'll hurt like hell.

"What a jerk," Brenner says, jaw throbbing. He tastes blood. He thinks a tooth is loose.

"Remember when he beat the crap out of that band geek? What's his name? Toby?" Jason opens another beer.

"Grade A, number one asshole," Brenner says.

A bulky guy in a camouflage jacket staggers past on the gravel shoulder and they both watch. Brenner's head spins from the beer and the dope.

"Hey, that him?" Jason points to the guy. "He thinks that jacket makes him somebody. Fuckin' Marines."

"He was a prick then and he's a prick now."

Brenner chugs his beer and tosses the can out the window. He jams the pickup into gear. Tires spin in the gravel and the truck swerves when the rubber grabs the road. Brenner stomps on the accelerator. The engine whines. Sean's in his sights.

"Teach him a lesson," Brenner says, ready to swerve at the last second, put the fear of God into that bastard.

"Jesus," says Jason. "No!" He grabs the wheel.

Brenner steers left; no time to explain it's a joke.

He smacked into a buck once, nearly totaled his mom's Cavalier. The impact is like that, maybe louder. Blood spatters the windshield.

As they speed into the dark, Brenner pounds on the dash. What has he done? He didn't mean to hit the guy, just wanted to scare him. Jason sticks his head out the window and looks back.

"It's not him," he shouts. "I don't think it's him. What if it's not him?"

Brenner drives faster, he can't think, and Jason vomits onto the floor of the truck.

"You're crazy," Jason yells. "Go back! I think you killed him."

Brenner runs a stop sign and then another, Jason shouting at him to go back, but when he gets to the light at Lee Highway just before the Interstate, he stops.

"This is bullshit," says Jason. He jumps out of the truck and runs.

"Good riddance," Brenner mutters. It wasn't his fault, anyway. It was an accident. Was it Sean? He's pretty sure it was. "The asshole deserved it."

He drives on. The smell of Jason's vomit is awful, like a skunk in the road, snaking down his throat, and his own stomach turns, but he opens the window and lets cool air batter his face. Then it's not so bad. He drinks more beer and that helps, too. He keeps driving.

He's on the edge of town, not far from Dora's place. He hasn't been there in a while. He stops out front, watching. It'll be light soon and he wonders what time the kid gets up, if there's a chance she'll let him see her. The truck idles rough and the rumble seems loud, loud enough to wake the neighborhood, so he drives away. The vomit smell is worse and he can't stop thinking that he's going to puke, too.

Under a street light he sees the blood on the hood, on the windshield. He tells himself Sean will be okay, that they weren't going fast, that somebody will find him and take care of him. But the blood tells a different story. Brenner's cheeks are wet, he's never done anything like this before, he's holding down the vomit, and now there's light in the sky.

He's near the high school. He thinks about ditching the truck, breaking into the school, trashing the gym, hiding there until he figures out what to do. He should go away, leave this hopeless town, he's got nothing here anyway. But that's no good. They'll know. Jason will talk, the faggot. Everyone will know.

He calls Dora on his cell phone. She'll know what to do. He can sleep there on the couch and see the kid in the morning and then all will be clear. But Dora doesn't answer. Why the fuck doesn't she answer?

He passes the school and now he's at Sean's folks' place. It's his truck in the driveway, it must be, with the fucking Semper Fi bumper sticker. Why is that truck here? Jason's vomit is finally too much and he can't stop his own from spilling out and he tries to open the door but it splashes on the window and his thigh and now he's out of the truck and kneeling by the front tire and the smell of rubber makes it worse and he heaves until there is no more. He stumbles to his feet, hands on the hood, and he sees the blood. Is it Sean's?

He needs to know, so he goes to the door. It's dawn, the birds are loud. He rings the bell. No one comes and he rings again. What difference does it make? He's killed someone, Sean or some other fucker.

He hears movement inside, a voice, and the door opens.

It's Sean. He's wearing a T-shirt and sweat pants, no blood, no injury. It wasn't him. It wasn't him. Jesus, what has he done?

Brenner thinks he might throw up again. He tries to look past Sean into the house, as if the other guy might be there, too. There's no one there. He doesn't know what to do, he's just killed somebody, maybe, fucked up big-time, and he has to do something to make it right. He looks up at Sean.

"My wrist," Brenner says. "You hurt my wrist. You're a fucking asshole."

Sean steps outside. "You woke me up to tell me that? You woke my parents up?" He pushes Brenner backward, moves with him.

"That's right, you bastard. You stupid, shit-for-brains bastard." Brenner pushes back as hard as he can and Sean fires a rocket into the center of Brenner's face. Blood gushes from his nose. His feeble swing at Sean is blocked and Sean hits him again and again, in the head and gut. Brenner goes down, but struggles to his feet.

"Bastard," Brenner says, already flagging. He can barely see now. "Stupid." Sean knees him in the groin and the pain is glorious, like the fucking sun exploding inside him. But he doesn't go down, he lunges at Sean again. "Stupid, stupid bastard."

A FIRE IN WINTER

Trace pulls the icy cap from his head, wraps it around his hand, and breaks the window. He clears the remaining shards of glass, reaches inside, twists the lock on the knob and pushes into the house. He's never done anything like this before, but what choice does he have in weather like this? He feels his way through the hallway, the only light a dim reflection from the snow-covered lawn. His hand touches a switch, but nothing happens. The house is cold and dank, but at least he's finally out of the wind and blowing snow.

His eyes adjust and now he can see more. There's a mirror in the entry, a dark hall leading to the left, the outline of a dining table and the emptiness of tall windows. Behind him a gust whistles through the broken pane in the door.

He takes the hallway to the right and stumbles over a chair, banging his knee on the floor as he falls. He flicks his lighter and steps further into the house. He comes to a room occupied only by a couch. He's suddenly tired. So very tired. He curls up, buries his head in the cushions, and sleeps.

He was lucky to find the house. When his mom's Grand Prix slid off the highway in heavy snow, pinning the door against a thick maple and sending a streaking crack across the windshield, he thought he might be dead. He'd been drinking, the tallboy of Bud flying from his hand as he tried to rein in the skid. He was in one piece, though, as far as he could tell. Nothing broken. He turned the key to restart the car, as if he might be able to drive out of his predicament, but the engine only shrieked and wouldn't start. He crawled across the seat to the passenger door, stumbled out, his feet slipping and sinking in the snow. There would be cars, he thought, someone would stop to help. But no one came, and the snow continued to fall.

He saw lights through the trees. Was it a house? Was it far? He moved into the woods, took a few steps and the lights disappeared. He kept on, and the lights came into view and faded again, and then they were gone. But he found the edge of the woods, a snowy lawn, an overgrown hedge, and the shadow of an enormous, dark house.

In the morning, hazy light filters into the room, and now he can see details. There is a rug over hardwood floors, faded, and worn in spots. The ceiling in this room is high and the walls are pale yellow, with streaks that might be dirt, or shadows. And there are pictures, paintings or prints he isn't yet sure which, in gilt frames that catch the dim light.

He finds a bathroom, surprised to have water, although what comes out of the tap is murky and frigid. He lets it run, hoping for warmth, but if anything the water seems to get colder. He splashes his face and wipes his hands on his jeans, still damp from the snow. There's a kitchen off the dining room, but the cupboards are empty. He's not hungry yet, but he will be.

"Where are you going?" Claudia shouted from her parents' porch.

He was half way to the car, surprised by how cold it had become. He didn't want to stop to answer her.

"Home," Trace said, fumbling with the keys. "This was a mistake."

"Daddy didn't mean it, honey."

"Of course he meant it, Claude."

"You're just going to leave me here?"

"Will you come?"

"You know I can't. They're my parents. Please come back inside. We'll talk to him together. It'll be fine. You'll see."

Trace slammed the car door shut, muffling her pleading voice.

♦ ♦ ♦

Now it's even colder and the snow has started again. The wind is fierce and the windows rattle. He wonders if the car has been found, if anyone knows what happened, if Claudia is looking for him. The snow is heavy. Even if he wanted to leave, he couldn't. There's no cell service. If he wanted to call her, he couldn't.

He explores the house. It's something to do, it helps him keep warm. It's huge. There are bedrooms upstairs, six or more, all empty. He finds the library downstairs. He's never been in a house with a library like this, all four walls lined floor to ceiling with filled shelves. He pulls out a book. *The Earth Speaks to Bryan.* It's a thin book, musty, the pages brittle and yellow. He reads a few pages, finds that the book is from 1925, an argument about evolution and the Scopes trial. He's heard of the trial, he thinks, but isn't sure what it was about, and isn't sure about evolution, either, which he thought was a new idea. He didn't know it had been around so long. He pulls out another book, this one even older, from 1906, *News from Nowhere.* And another, older still, from 1873. Why are they here? What is this place?

Now he's hungry, and needs to find something to eat. He re-checks the kitchen. He might need to eat the books, a bookworm, he thinks, and laughs, and wonders how bad it would have to get for him to really do that. He's hungry, *and* he's cold.

He's back on the sofa, with a copy of *Gone with the Wind* he's pulled from the library. He's heard of this one, but thought it was a movie. He isn't sure what it's about. He opens it and reads the first page. The wind howls—he laughs again, thinking about the wind and the title of the book—and the house shudders. He looks up from the book and notices the fireplace.

All the way from DC, Claudia had seemed tense. She had something to say, he knew that's what it meant when she chewed her lip like that, formulating her argument, hunting for the words.

"Spit it out, Claudia. Or are you going to make me guess again." She did that sometimes, testing his ability to read her, to determine if they were suited for each other despite their different backgrounds. He laughed and took his eyes off the swirling snow to see if she smiled, if his laughter had loosened her up at all. A gust of wind pulled his gaze back to the road.

"My parents," she said and stopped.

Out of the corner of his eye he saw that she had looked away, was staring out the side window at the sugar-dusted fields.

"Your parents," he said. "What about your parents?"

She settled a hand on his leg. "They don't know."

"Which part don't they know? That we're getting married? Or that I'm white?"

"They don't know," she said.

It's dark again, the winter day ending early. The cold is painful now, his fingers numb. The thought of nibbling on a book occurs to him again, not quite as funny this time, and he sees the fireplace once more. He can't eat the books, but maybe they'll burn. He opens the book in his hands—it's dry and brittle—and sets it in the fireplace grate. He reaches inside and opens the flue with a yank. He holds his lighter to a page that flutters in the draft and the flame consumes the page, then engulfs the rest. He rubs his hands before the fire and for a moment he is warm. He runs to the library and grabs more books, a Jack London, a Hemingway. He opens them both and sets them on the fire.

He remembers something from high school days, about book burning and censorship. His own mother had joined a protest at his school, something she didn't think he should be allowed to read. He doesn't even remember what it was now, or what harm she thought it would do. He grabs another book: *The Klansman*. Inside there's a drawing of a guy wearing a white robe and a pointy hat. This one he understands. He drops it into the fire.

It was Trace's idea to make the trip. Claudia had finally agreed to marry him, and he wanted to meet her parents, who lived in Southwestern Virginia. She resisted. They couldn't afford the trip, she said, her car would never make it, they both had exams, the weather was so unpredictable at that time of year, her parents worked and were always busy with this and that. But it was only gas, they had enough money for that, and his mother would lend him her car. After all, she was as hard-nosed as they came and even she had come around, eventually, and liked the idea once she got used to it. And she loved Claude.

"I bet they're dying to meet the man in your life. Aren't they? Their future son-in-law?"

She didn't answer. He wanted to know why. And finally she gave in.

He finds an encyclopedia in the library. It has 21 volumes. It's old, but newer than the other books and the pages are thicker; it doesn't burn as readily, which he realizes is a good thing for his purposes. It also doesn't throw off as much heat, but it will last longer. The pages blacken and curl before they sprout yellow flames, and he can almost read them while they burn, "Archaeology is the study of . . ." He stacks the whole set on the hearth, like logs.

He has to eat something and wishes he'd paid more attention when he was a cub scout. Did they even talk about survival back then, did they have to identify berries and nuts? He doesn't want to go outside, but there's no choice.

He pulls the hat over his ears, tugs his jacket tight, and braves the wind. There's at least a foot of snow, drifting across the lawn, and he isn't sure what he might find, or where to look. But there has to be something. Briefly, he considers finding the road, a store, a passing car, getting to a phone and calling Claudia's house, asking for help even if he has to talk to her father. But even if that made sense in this weather, he can't do it. He's making a point, although he's no longer sure what it is.

The woods behind the house hold promise. The snow isn't as deep here, but he still doesn't see anything edible. He tramps around between the trees. He doesn't see them, but feels something hard and round under his feet. He kicks the snow away and finds brown, golf-ball-sized nuts. Walnuts, he guesses, but isn't sure. He gathers a dozen and fills his pockets. How many is enough? He isn't sure of that either. And what else does he need? What else can he eat?

Back in the house he tries to open the nuts. He breaks the husk, and his fingers darken, black, even darker than Claudia's fingers, which are pale, coffee-with-milk. The tannin bites at his nose, a smell of the woods. He's left with a hard shell, impenetrable.

Trace saw Claudia in a blues club in Adams Morgan and recognized her from one of his classes at GW. He watched her come in, his eyes drawn to her tight, black curls and tight, black jeans, the graceful rhythm of her step, dancing across the room instead of walking. He followed her to the bar and paid for her beer.

She wouldn't return his calls, but he persisted. She wouldn't go out with him, but he kept asking. She wouldn't come up to his place, and when she finally relented, she left after one drink. When she came back a week later, and they tumbled into bed, she wouldn't stay. For months he begged her to move in. Eventually she did.

The encyclopedia keeps burning, but doesn't do enough to combat the cold. He pulls books from the shelves at random: *Three Men in a Boat*, from 1889, is ashes in minutes; *The Story of the Typewriter*, from 1923, lasts a bit longer.

His stomach aches from hunger. He sits in front of the fire and sets one of the walnuts on the stone hearth, taking aim with Volume X-Z of the encyclopedia. He raises the book over his head and slams it onto the nut, which is unharmed by the blow. He examines the book, his fingers brushing over the dent in its cover. He finds an old atlas and slams the nut again, with the same result. He considers pulling a plank from the bookshelf in the library, but the shelves are built-in, immovable. He searches the kitchen, pulling out drawer after drawer, hoping for a hammer, or anything. But there's nothing, and then he remembers seeing rocks bordering the garden just outside the door. He retrieves one.

He settles another book on the fire and attacks a nut with the stone. The first blow does nothing, but he hears the nut crack on the second try. He brings the rock down again and shards fly across the room. He retrieves the fragments and digs out the meat of the nut, a bitter, hard kernel between his teeth. He eats all he can find and then it's gone, hardly worth the trouble, but it's something. He attacks another and another and he eats all the walnuts, then goes out where he found them and gets some more and eats those.

He decides that red books burn better than others, so he grabs an arm load, another London, a Faulkner, a Joyce, and throws them on the fire.

The snow had started while they were still on I-81 with another couple of hours to go before they reached Claudia's parents' house. Trace now understood from her silence that her parents didn't know she was engaged and, more to the point, didn't know that her boyfriend was white. So there was going to be some awkwardness to start with, maybe. But they'd get over it, surely? She loved him, so why wouldn't they?

"There's a reason you didn't tell them, isn't there?" he said. Despite the snow, the road was in good shape and traffic was moving fast. His mom's car had all kinds of power and he enjoyed driving it through the mountains.

"All right," she said. "Here it is. My father has a problem with whites. He's from a different time and place. He came up from Georgia as a boy. He remembers how it was."

"I get that it was bad," Trace said. "But it's not like that anymore, is it? Plus, this is me, not some Georgia cracker."

"There's more, though."

Trace took his eyes off the road for a second to look at her and felt the Grand Prix swerve into the left lane. He slowed and steered back. "Tell me."

"Okay." She took a deep breath. "It's my mother. When I was about five—we lived near Blacksburg then—she was raped. By a white man. My father can't forgive something like that."

He sleeps fitfully. The wind howls, but the snow has stopped. He can see the moon through the bare windows, its reflected light bright on the snow. In the morning, the sky is clear. His stomach aches, but he no longer feels hungry. This can't go on much longer, though. He has to leave. He tosses the last of the encyclopedia volumes on the fire, but glowing ash leaps from the grate and drifts up, coming to rest on the rug. He envisions the rug bursting into flames, taking the house with it, and he imagines how warm he'd be in the center of the fire, with nothing left to worry about. He steps on the ash, extinguishing the flame before it begins.

They finally arrived at the house in mid-afternoon, a white-clapboard cottage on a quiet road. You can tell a lot about people from how they keep their yard, Trace thought. The Crawfords' yard was orderly, with trimmed bushes along the driveway, a flower bed in front of the house, like a moat. The mother's doing? Or the father? They cared what the neighbors thought. They liked things just so.

The snow was heavier now, settling on the Grand Prix as they climbed out and headed to the door. Claudia's mother, a petite woman wearing jeans and a red sweater, her hair short like Claudia's, greeted her with a tight hug, but her eyes were on Trace. The father, tall with a barrel chest, stood behind his wife, glowering at Trace.

"Who is that?" he said gruffly.

"Come inside, Trace, it's freezing out here," Claudia said. "Daddy, this is Trace."

Trace stepped up to the door, Claudia and her mother having moved further inside, but her father blocked the way.

"I don't care who he is, little girl. He's not welcome in my house."

"Daddy, please. Let me explain. Trace, get in here."

But the man was so large, he filled the doorway, and Trace couldn't enter.

"Howard, let the man in," the mother said.

He took a step back, as if relenting, and Trace moved forward, eager to get out of the snow. When he had only one foot inside, Claudia's father put both hands on Trace's chest and shoved, sending Trace flying off the stoop.

"Boy, if I catch you sniffing around my daughter again I will kill your sorry white ass. Do you hear me?" From behind the door he pulled out a shotgun that he now aimed at Trace.

"Daddy!" Claudia screamed, as Trace scrambled off the lawn and back to the Grand Prix.

He has no idea where he is. When he left Claudia's parents' house, he just drove. He'd stopped at a convenience store where he got the beer, but from there he kept going, unable to judge direction in the snow. Now that the storm is over, he'll have to go for help. But where?

As he pulls on his jacket and cap, he takes a last look around the house. He realizes how old it must be. He's no judge of these things—growing up in DC, what does he know about big old country houses?—but he guesses it's from before the Civil War. A plantation house, then, home to rich white people. Probably people who owned slaves.

High school feels like a long time ago now, but he remembers studying about slavery. He went to public school in DC and there were lots of black kids in his class. The teachers—mostly white, but there were black teachers, too—tiptoed around the subject. Instead of telling the students what to think about slavery, they let the kids talk it through. That was an eye-opener. He'd had no idea. Some of his own friends, teammates on the basketball team, descended from slaves, with stories they'd heard passed down from generation to generation. Horror stories. They'd read a book about it he remembered, *Beloved*. It wasn't even that long ago.

No wonder Claudia's father was angry. But it wasn't Trace. It wasn't even Trace's ancestors, Irish immigrants who came later, after the war. But Trace gets it. Or, he supposes, he can't really *get* it, but he doesn't blame the man. And what happened to her mother? Man, that shouldn't happen to anybody.

Trace trudges through the snow, away from the house. The road hasn't been plowed yet, and stretches white and empty in both directions. Looking one way, he sees the Grand Prix, a snow-covered lump in a ditch, leaning against the leafless tree. The other way, back the way he came, is

Claudia's house and the convenience store. He'll make his way to the store, call her. He'll apologize for running. They'll figure something out, some way to make it all right with her father.

He looks back at the house, a stately mansion from this distance, not the rundown husk he knows it to be. The windows appear to be glowing yellow in the morning light. Is it a reflection of the sun, or something else?

Part IV: Midwestern Gothic

COUSIN BARNABY IS DEAD

I'm in the middle of an argument with my mother—she thinks I should ask her friend's daughter Denise Knickerbocker out on a date while I'm home for spring break, and I think that's the worst idea ever—when the phone rings. I want her to let the answering machine get it, or make Dad answer it, wherever he is, in their bedroom or the basement or sneaking a smoke on the back porch, because I want her to listen to me for a change. Instead, she glances at the caller ID and lifts the receiver.

After "Hello," she's silent, nods solemnly as if the caller can see her and will understand that she's taking whatever it is seriously. Then it's "Yes," "Yes," "I'm so sorry," and she hangs up. She looks at me and there are tears in her eyes.

"Cousin Barnaby is dead." She says this with resignation in her voice, as if the news is inevitable.

I don't know what to say. It doesn't seem possible. The guy's my age, but he's *her* first cousin, the son of her mother's younger sister. The first time I met him was at a family reunion in Cleveland that I did *not* want to go to and neither did he. We were maybe twelve at the time. I was missing basketball camp back home in Indianapolis and Barn—he liked to be called Barn, but his parents insisted on the whole dumb name that made him sound like a circus clown—was into hanging out with his friends at the mall in Pittsburgh. So we were both there against our wills. Another time was here in Indy just a couple of years ago when Barn and his mother came to visit. I think she was getting a divorce or something and wanted to hide out for a while. I remember there was a big hubbub because Barn's older brother Bailey didn't come with them. He was supposed to be some hotshot college guy, which back then seemed like a big deal. It was cool that he didn't come, though, because Barn brought some pot he stole from Bailey's bedroom, and we smoked out in the woods behind our house. He talked about Hermann Hesse and alienation and duality and more shit that was way over my head. I thought he was cool.

Cousin Barnaby is dead. Shit.

"How?" I ask my mother.

She doesn't answer.

Even though we didn't see each other much, now that I'm thinking about him I feel pretty bad that he's dead. I don't know anyone my age who's dead, except this kid in high school who had some horrible disease and scooted around the school in an electric wheelchair so no one would feel guilty about not wanting to talk to him. So I didn't *really* know him. When he died, the school set up a scholarship in his name. I didn't hear who got the scholarship—other kids in wheelchairs, maybe.

"Never mind, Robbie" my mother says, finally, like she's been thinking all this time of what lie to tell me.

If she doesn't want to talk about it, I'm guessing either Barn killed himself, which doesn't seem possible, or maybe somebody killed him, and either way it sucks. It's lame that she won't tell me, but typical for her. My folks think I'm still a kid and can't handle the truth.

I must have rolled my eyes then because she does an about-face, which is pretty unusual for her.

"If you must know, it was an accident. He was driving his little Korean car or Yugo or whatever and he crashed. Died instantly. Are you happy now?"

Of course I'm not happy. What a crazy thing to say! That would be creepy under any circumstances, although I *am* glad she decided to tell me, which says something about where we are in our relationship. Maybe it's because I'm a college man now. We're making progress.

Anyway, our argument is over now thanks to Barn. I can see she's forgotten about Denise Knickerbocker, and instead she's thinking about how awful her aunt must feel and what a relief it is that it happened to her pothead cousin and not her own son. She doesn't notice that I'm holding on to the back of a chair so I don't fall over. I can't believe Barn is dead. I didn't even know he had a car.

The real reason I don't want to ask Denise out, by the way, and the reason we were arguing in the first place, is because of the nickname some guys used to call her behind her back: DeNeeds Biggerknockers. After I heard that once, I couldn't even look at her, never mind go out on a date with her. Can you imagine trying to feel her up and having that name come to mind? I wouldn't be able to keep a straight face.

But now, after Mom's shocker, there *is* somebody I want to see. This girl named Corinne Ackerman had a huge crush on Barn, the kind where you write somebody love poems and send them emails and threaten to do terrible things to yourself if they don't write back. She met him when he was here that one time and I think they might have made out when I wasn't around. I'm pretty sure they stayed in touch after that, because once when I talked to Barn on the phone he mentioned he could have Corinne any time he wanted. He even talked about what he'd like to do with her. It was kind of crude, but funny. Anyway, I figure she's home for Spring break just like I am, and this is news she'd want to have.

After dinner, my folks start talking about driving to Pittsburgh for Barn's funeral, which seems like the worst thing imaginable. I mean, I really liked the guy, like I said, and it's sad and everything that he got killed, but there's no way I'm going to his funeral and looking into a coffin at his dead face. He was a good looking kid, you know, and when he said those things about having sex with Corinne any time he wanted, he wasn't joking. And not just Corinne, but any girl he set his sights on. I don't want to even think about going to the funeral.

So I tell my parents I'm meeting some buddies—we're all home for Spring break and we're going to hang out, I say, although the truth is a bunch of them went to Cabo or someplace and I'm stuck here in Indianapolis where there's still snow on the ground. Besides I'm not really in the mood for hanging out with guys who didn't know Barn. Instead, I head over to Corinne Ackerman's.

Corinne's mom is shocked to see me because it's been a couple of years, but after a double-take she invites me in and says what a nice surprise and Corinne will be so happy. Then she calls down the hall. Speaking of surprises, I'm floored when Corinne comes out. I used to think Barn was making fun of her when he talked about doing it with her because she was kind of chubby when we were younger. Now she's incredibly skinny. Like way too skinny.

We sit in the living room and Corinne's mom serves us Coke and pretzels—although what I really want at this point is a beer—and says again what a nice surprise it is to see me.

"How's Barnaby?" Corinne asks as soon as we're alone, and I can tell she hasn't gotten over the thing she had for him, and it might not be so easy to tell her what I've come to tell her.

"You home for break?" I ask, because that's what my dad does. Whenever I ask a question he doesn't want to answer, he just asks another question.

"No," she says. "I mean, I'm on break, but I didn't go away. I'm in school here."

Corinne was near the top of our class, took all the advanced courses. I figured she'd have gone to Harvard or someplace. Notre Dame, at least.

"That's convenient," I say.

"So how's Barnaby?" she asks again.

I sip the Coke, munch a couple of pretzels. I can hear the TV going in the living room where her mom is, some sitcom with a loud laugh track.

"That's the thing, Cor," I say, putting on this fake nickname-closeness I don't really feel, "I've got some bad news about Barn."

The color leaves her face, and I can see her shoulders stiffen, like she's preparing to get slugged. I reach for another pretzel, but there's no way I can stop now. So I just say it.

"Barnaby is dead."

It starts slowly, so there's time for her to put down her drink, but she begins to shake all over. First her head trembles, and then I see her long hair kind of dancing around on her shoulders because her whole body is quivering. Her hand flies to her mouth and she's bending over like she's going to vomit. She jumps off the couch and runs to the bathroom, and I can hear it, probably what little dinner she ate is coming back up. Of course she knows all about puking, I figure, so for her this is probably no big deal.

When I go to tell Mrs. Ackerman that Corinne's sick, she's already standing outside the bathroom looking tired, like she's done this one too many times. I can hear Corinne inside sobbing and puking, so I tell her mom that I have to go, and I get out of there as fast as I can. Telling her was supposed to make me feel better, but instead I feel a hundred times worse.

I can't go home, though. I told my folks I'm hanging out with buddies, and it's too early for that to be over. And, besides, I don't want to hear any more about the funeral or that Barn must have been doing drugs, or whatever. So I walk around the neighborhood for a while. It's nothing special, nothing but single-story ranch houses, pretty much the same as when I was a kid. I get in the car and drive past our house once to check, and the lights are still on, so I go on down to the McDonald's near the Interstate, which is just about the lamest thing I could possibly do, and I eat a hamburger I don't even want, try not to think about Barn, and then drive around some more. When I make another pass by the house it's dark, so I figure it's safe to head in.

When I get to my room, I'm feeling pretty low. For one thing, seeing Corinne was weird. She's obviously got some problems, but I didn't think she'd take the news about Barn that hard. Or maybe I did, and that's why I went over there. But the thing that bothers me is that it hit her way harder than it did me, and he's my cousin for Christ's sake. But, now that I think about it, the whole thing does really suck, and I wish Barn weren't dead. I never got to tell him I thought he was cool and, you know, that I liked him. Not that he cared what his dorky cousin from Indiana thought, but still. And then, out of no place, I start to cry. Not like Corinne, who was completely out of control, but a few tears sneak out of the corners of my eyes and run down my cheeks.

After a while the tears stop, but I'm not sure they're gone for good, like when you think you've put an end to a spell of hiccups, but back they come.

And then I think of this guy Roy I know at school. We were shooting the breeze one day in the dorm cafeteria and I found out he's from Pittsburgh, so I asked him if he knew Barnaby Mackintosh. "Sure I know him," he said. It turns out they went to the same high school. So, mostly because he knew Barn and even claimed to be friends with him, I started hanging out with Roy sometimes. He's a pretty good guy—smart but not so smart he makes you feel bad about yourself, pretty interested in girls but not so successful that you feel like a loser around him. That's Roy. I really want to talk to someone about Barn and how I feel about him. That's the real reason I went over to see Corinne, I realize, but that hadn't gone so well. If I could talk to Roy and we could both tell each other what a great guy Barn was, then we'll make ourselves feel better and we'll be honoring Barn in some way too, and that'll be better than some lousy funeral any day.

The phone's in the living room, so I go back out there. It takes awhile to get his folks' number from directory assistance, but then I call. It's late and I'm worried about that, but it's not something that's going to wait until tomorrow, not the way I'm feeling, so I let the phone ring and ring and finally somebody picks it up.

"Roy," I say, because I recognize his voice. "It's Robbie. How're you doing?"

Great, he says, or something like that, but honestly I'm not listening. I'm figuring out what I'm going to say next, and I'm trying really hard not to cry.

"Look, Roy, the reason I'm calling is I just heard that my cousin Barnaby is dead."

There's silence on his end of the line and I figure the news is sinking in. I know it's a tough thing to hear.

"No, he's not," says Roy. He's in denial. Totally understandable. I'm about to lose it again myself.

"Yeah, he is," I say. "Somebody called my mom. He had an accident or something. Barn's dead."

"I'm telling you he's not. I *just* saw him at a party. He was getting seriously wasted because his brother got killed in a wreck. It's Bailey that's dead, man. Not Barn."

Holy shit. Did my mom confuse the names? Did she mean Bailey, not Barnaby? Or did whoever called her get it wrong? Did I hear it wrong?

The first thing I think of is Corinne. I've never seen anyone so hung up on another person, and I guess she had problems of her own to deal with besides. People like that are on the edge, you know? But maybe it's okay. When I left her house she was with her mom. She probably talks stuff over with her, not like me and my mom, and if the news of Barn's death upset her that bad her mother would help her out.

Even so, I have to tell her about the mix-up. Only I don't want my folks to hear the car starting up again, and since it's just a couple of blocks away I head outside. It's cold as hell, and I don't have a jacket on, but I don't want to take the time to go back inside and get one, so I just start jogging and figure I'll warm up pretty quick.

And as I'm running, I feel myself start to smile, laugh even, because cousin Barnaby isn't dead after all. It was just a crazy mix-up with my mom. I feel bad about Bailey, of course, but I hardly even knew him, and I'm thinking that tomorrow I'll call Barn in Pittsburgh, and I guess I won't tell him what happened but I'll tell him how sorry I am about his brother and stuff, and it will be great to hear his voice. Maybe we can meet up this summer, spend some time together.

So I'm running down the street, I'm grinning and pretty happy about how things have turned out considering how shitty I felt a little while ago, and I'm watching the road because like I said it's cold and there's snow on the ground and black icy patches on the pavement that will send me flying if I hit one. And that's why I don't see the ambulance in front of Corinne's house until I'm practically on top of it. It's a wonder how I could have missed it, because the red light on top is spinning and flashing and spreading that eerie light all over the neighborhood.

I look up and I see Corinne's mom standing in their doorway. She's crying and her hand is covering her mouth, and there's some man standing there with her like he's asking questions. I know, as sure as I know anything, what happened.

And I also know that I am the last person Mrs. Ackerman wants to see right now. So I just keep on running, past the ambulance, past the house, through the cold dark neighborhood of my childhood, in the spooky glow of that flashing light.

ADJUNCT

Lorenzo takes the call when Sandy buzzes him on the intercom, even though he's with new clients. Their estate plan is a simple matter—matching wills, a trust—and the elderly couple can wait. They might even be impressed that the law school Dean is on the line. It's a small town, after all, dominated by the university, and the old lady is a talker. Word will get around that the new guy from Chicago is connected. More fees down the road, if he plays his cards right. His dad will be pleased. The law firm of Rossi & Rossi is soaring.

The Dean—Frankie—has been a buddy of his ever since their first-year Contracts class in law school, in which they competed for the attention of the petite brunette professor, each trying to outdo the other with his analysis of Taylor v. Caldwell, or Hadley v. Baxendale. They were drawn to one another, two out-of-place Italian kids in the Midwest ("Like wings on a pig," Frankie used to say) and looked enough alike—dark, gangly, slicked-back hair—that they were sometimes mistaken for brothers, an error they didn't always correct. They competed, too, in cutthroat games of handball, punishing matches that left them both bloody and breathless. Through summer internships, bar exam prep classes and stints as tireless robots in Chicago mega-firms, they hung out, overindulged, commiserated, and celebrated triumphs, both professional and venereal. Frankie was best man in Lorenzo's first wedding, Lorenzo a groomsman in Frankie's only. They were tight.

Tight, that is, until Frankie's first book (he somehow became an expert in the esoteric but suddenly hot field of eminent domain for private purposes) followed by his departure from Chicago and subsequent academic stardom at their alma mater. It's natural that friends, even brothers, would drift apart, come back together. The same thing happened for a time in law school, when Frankie was selected for the prestigious law review and Lorenzo was not. He wasn't happy about being left behind, but he didn't hold it against Frankie. Still doesn't. He understands. They just aren't as much alike as either of them once believed. That's all. Even now that he has returned to Bloomington to join his father's law practice, which he did in part because his buddy Frankie is here, they rarely see each other. They're in different worlds. They're both older, busier. No big deal.

"Frankie, you old son-of-a-gun," Lorenzo practically shouts into the phone, winking at the couple parked in ox-blood wing chairs opposite his cluttered desk. It occurs to him that the call wouldn't need to be legit to have the desired effect; it's working already. He can see the sparkle in the woman's eyes, her ears cocked for any tidbit she might later repeat in her sewing circle or book club. He'd have to talk to Sandy about this, work out a signal for her to patch through some made-up dignitary when there's a trophy catch in the office, a hook that needs to be set. 'What can I do you for?' He straightens his tie and winks at the old folks again.

Frankie apologizes for not calling more often since Lorenzo's come back to town. A busy time at the law school, he says, and Lorenzo is inclined to believe him. The truth is it's been a disappointment to Lorenzo, although he's confessed that to no one. Who would he tell? To make it up to him, Frankie invites him to sit in on a class and consider showing up each week as "Practitioner-In-Residence," a program Frankie initiated after taking over as Dean. It will give them a chance to catch up.

Lorenzo watches the old couple pretending to study the diplomas on the wall, his bar admission certificates, his tickets, he once believed, to fame and fortune. Or fortune, at least. But not academics. Whatever he may once have shared with Frankie, in this way they were never much alike. Frankie loves the law, its intricacies and history, thrives in its back alleys and secret passageways. Lorenzo is honest enough with himself to admit he merely loves what the law can do for him. That's what those pieces of paper on the wall mean. He likes trolling for business, arguing with opposing counsel and billing time and expenses on clients' accounts. He thrives in an Armani suit, feels powerful behind the wheel of his Z-4. That's the law for him, that's what matters. Not research and teaching, not fusty books. Besides, he's a busy man. He has his cases, prospective clients to schmooze, his father looking over his shoulder at the office, his kids every other weekend. Not to mention two ex-wives and, lately, high-maintenance Maya, who takes up most of his time and all of his energy.

"I don't know, Frankie," says Lorenzo, forgetting for a moment the presence of his clients.

"You could share your expertise with the students," Frankie insists. "You'd have way more credibility than a mere teacher. Even me. I've been away from the trenches too long. You're the real deal. They'll love you."

His father bellows on the phone in the next office, a sour divorce case, his dad's bread and butter. The old couple fidgets; Lorenzo flashes a mollifying grin. How did these two stay together so long? He wonders, not for the first time, how his own parents managed it, or Frankie and his wife. How can anyone these days still take "Till death do you part" seriously when there are so many distractions?

"Plus," Frankie goes on, "think how great it'll sound when you're pitching new clients: Lorenzo Rossi, Adjunct Professor of Law." He knows Frankie has played his trump card, that this is the argument he won't be able to resist. And Frankie's not wrong. Like no one else, Frankie knows how to push his buttons.

Despite the new stationery his father has ordered and the fresh gold lettering on the office door, Rossi & Rossi, Lorenzo views the arrangement with his father as temporary, a base camp for a renewed assault on the mountain. After the incident at his last firm—he had bounced around to six or seven outfits, more than most lawyers, looking for his niche, he said whenever anyone remarked on the frequent moves—getting out of the city seemed like a good idea. It wasn't the first time he'd slept with an intern, even when he was still married, but it was the first time one had claimed sexual harassment. She did it to guarantee herself a job offer after graduation, he knew, a shrewd ploy he had to respect. But the damage was severe. Even if he'd landed a spot in another decent firm, doubtful given his employment history and the viral news of his indiscretion, he couldn't bear to run into his former colleagues, a certainty in the surprisingly small Chicago legal community.

No one here knows the whole, humiliating story, and he's not inclined to open up. Not to his father. Not to Frankie. Certainly not to Maya, who couldn't possibly understand. It was a blow, sure, an episode he'd like to forget. But it would pass, the wounds would heal, and in a couple of years it would be erased from the collective memory like a bad dream. He'd be back, in fighting trim. In the meantime, this was as good a place as any to wait.

On top of which, his father, a long-time solo-practitioner who pushed him toward law school in the first place, said he needed the help, that there was more than enough work to go around, and that life in the sticks wasn't so bad, that it would grow on him. And with his mother not long gone, the battle with a rare cancer taking a toll on them both, his dad was lonely. So, he came and here he is. He's making the best of it. But the gig at the law school could be just what he needed: the first step back to the big time.

It's an early class, and his eyes barely focus when Frankie introduces him to Hal, the young professor he'll be assisting. A clueless nerd, he assesses: never spent a day in the real world, wouldn't know a billable hour if it bit him in the ass. No wonder Frankie begged. These kids really do need him. As the students settle into their seats—it's a typical law school classroom, desks tiered theater-style so everyone is visible to the teacher, no place to hide—Frankie lingers, watching. It brings back memories for Lorenzo, seeing these students and being here with Frankie. There was a girl in one of their classes, he remembers, Criminal Procedure he thinks, who wasn't interested in either one of them. They turned it into a contest, a beer bet, to see who could get Lesley to go out with him. It took all semester, but he wishes he had a picture of Frankie's face when he and Lesley strolled into Nick's Pub one night, the wager won. They laughed about it for weeks. Whatever happened to those days?

Hal begins class and Frankie leaves, glancing over his shoulder as he goes. Lorenzo takes a front row seat, sips his no-foam latte, plots what to say when called upon, just like the bad old Socratic days of law school, calculates the income he's losing by being there. No way he can do this every week. Not even for Frankie.

He hears his name, looks up from his coffee, and Hal beckons. At the podium, he leans forward, studies faces. The bitter coffee aroma clashes with his own lemony aftershave. He looks at his watch. He bumped his nine o'clock meeting to ten, a possible medical malpractice case, outside his professional comfort zone, but a potential goldmine. Frankie owes him.

"I took this class when I was here," he begins, addressing a wide-eyed geek in the first row: destined for law review, needs to get laid. His eyes link with a sleepy jock, slouched in his chair near the back, wrinkled T-shirt and chin stubble: hung-over and horny, man after my own heart. The thought makes him smile with the memory of early classes missed, notes borrowed from Frankie. "Best decision I ever made," he says. Older woman on the aisle, heavy, floral dress: isn't she the librarian? "Provides me a very comfortable living." God, why did I agree to do this? Tough guy on the aisle, Marine hair, a high-and-tight: is his sleeve pinned to his shoulder?

There are questions. He finds more faces while the front-row geek asks about the desirability of generation-skipping trusts: man, what a loser. A black woman in dreadlocks: headed for legal aid. A fat girl who looks like Sandy, his dad's tireless secretary. A skinny kid—buttoned down, rep tie: a shoo-in at some snooty law firm. Lorenzo ventures an answer to the geek's question, but stops mid-bullshit. There, in the middle of the classroom, is a breathtaking blond, tall, fresh, busty. She doesn't even look real to him. She's perfect, provocative. Centerfold material. The kind of girl he never gets to see anymore, what with work, his dad, the kids. Maya.

The girl smiles. Her teeth gleam. Is it his imagination or can he actually smell her sweet, cinnamon breath from where he stands? He studies Hal's seating chart on the podium. Even her name is perfect: Ingrid.

He straightens his tie, stands tall. Adjunct Professor has a nice ring to it. Maybe Frankie was right, maybe this is going to be good for him. He loves the law.

He drops into Frankie's office to give him the news.

"If you really need me," Lorenzo says, "I guess I can squeeze this in."

"Great," Frankie says. He gets up and closes the door. "There's just one thing, buddy. This isn't Chicago, if you know what I mean."

"I can't say that I do. Buddy."

"This may be the sticks, 'Enzo, but word gets around."

Filled floor-to-ceiling bookcases line Frankie's office. Lorenzo recognizes his old friend's own treatise, sees how comfortably it sits among all the rest. "What's your point?" he asks.

Frankie's arms are folded across his chest. "Nothing," he says. "No point."

The next week, Lorenzo arrives early and lingers outside the classroom as the students filter in. The geek. The frat boy. The librarian. When there's no sign of Ingrid, he realizes he's made a colossal mistake, that he's committed to a semester of early morning pain, not to mention lost income, all for nothing, for a glimpse of a beauty who isn't even in the class. She was only an auditor. Or she dropped the class. Or . . . and then she turns the corner, a notebook and the thick text pressed against her chest as she strolls alongside the one-armed Marine, whose cane-aided gait is painful to watch.

From where he sits in the classroom he can observe the girl: note-taking; whispering to the Marine; leaning toward nerdy Hal; concentrating on whatever it is that he's lecturing about, the formalities of instrument execution. Excruciating stuff. It's what paralegals are for, not something these kids really have to master, but Hal is too cloistered to know that. Twice Ingrid looks his way and then, when their eyes meet, stares down at her notebook. Is she blushing? When Hal dismisses the class, Ingrid is the first out the door.

That's the pattern. She arrives late, just before Hal begins the lecture, and is the first to leave. He hopes for a chance to talk, to invite her for coffee. He has it all worked out. He'll tell her there's an opening for a clerkship in his firm—he'll flash one of the new cards, Lorenzo Rossi, Partner, Rossi & Rossi—and that she should apply. She'll be impressed, flattered, and will come to the office for an interview, another chance to be alone with her, the only candidate. And, even if his father doesn't agree that they need a student around the office, at least he'll have made a connection. Hell, he could hire her out of his own pocket, a few bucks an hour, chump change, regardless of what the old man thinks. But if he can't even talk to the girl, if she's forever elusive, his plan won't get off the ground, much less fly.

He has lunch one day with Frankie and it feels great to be back together. They've spoken a few times at school and Frankie hasn't mentioned Chicago again. Things are going great. It's Friday and they're both loose, they have a couple of beers with their burgers at Nick's just like old times. Lorenzo asks about Frankie's wife, Melinda, a middle-school teacher. Lorenzo went out with her for a few months up in Chicago, between marriages and shortly before Frankie met her, although he's never confessed that to Frankie.

"She's fine," Frankie says.

He waits for more but Frankie doesn't expand. He remembers Melinda as pale and soft, breasts pendulous. Adventurous in the sack. He can't quite picture her face.

"What about you?" Frankie asks. "How're all your ex-wives? How's that new babe?" He's grinning, and Lorenzo has never felt so good about being back in town. For once, it feels right. The trouble in Chicago is ancient history. It's great to be with his old friend, his almost-brother. Frankie's beating him out for law review is old news. Being snubbed when Frankie made it big—it's in the past. They're reunited now; life is good. And now it's time to get to the point of the lunch.

"What's the story with that Marine in my class?" Sometimes the best approach to what you want is through the back door. A little misdirection. Don't want to give away too much. An old lawyer's trick.

"Army, actually. As I understand it, he got hit by a roadside bomb patrolling Baghdad. A good man."

"And the blond girl who hangs out with him, Ingrid?"

Frankie looks up from his burger, finishes chewing, sips his beer. "A blond? I think I know who you mean. What about her?"

"What's her story? Is she sleeping with the Marine?" He knows now the student's not a Marine, but the nickname he's assigned is too firmly engrained. It helps to keep the man in a box, out of his thoughts. "Are they a couple?"

Frankie laughs. "Hate to disappoint you, but, contrary to popular belief, the Dean does not keep track of all sexual activity in the school." He finishes his beer and glances over his shoulder, turns back and lowers his head and his voice as if he's about to reveal a deep, dark secret. "Didn't Chicago teach you anything?"

Two months into the semester, he has a dinner date with Maya. Usually they go to Malibu Grill on the Courthouse Square—Maya sometimes works there as a cocktail waitress, that's how they met—or to the chophouse out by the Mall. But for this outing he's reserved a table, the one up front, right by the window, at La Cucina, the Italian café across the street from the law school.

"Why here?" Maya asks. "We never come here." She tosses her slate-black bangs out of her eyes. As she slides into her chair she holds out her arm and admires the silver bracelet he's just given her, the one she gazed at in the window of Zales the week before, wide and heavy and inset with gaudy turquoise. He's never been one to give expensive gifts, not even when panged by guilt, and, besides, he hasn't done anything. Yet. But lately when they're together, especially during sex, his mind has been elsewhere, and the actual cheating—always inevitable—is now only a formality. The bracelet isn't an apology, exactly; it's more like a message from his future unfaithful self, one she'll only later be able to interpret.

"Bingo," he says. "A change." That, and the fact it's a law school favorite and he hopes Ingrid might come in or, at least, stroll by.

Their salads are limp, the breadsticks stale. Maya's pasta is overdone and—she insists he try it, shoving a forkful into his mouth—the marinara is tasteless. His scaloppini is dry and tough. They sip espressos and share a bland tiramisu. All through dinner he's kept an eye on the restaurant door, and also on the entrance to the law school, waiting to catch sight of Ingrid. He feels sorry for Maya, in a way. It isn't her fault. It can't be helped.

He's paying the check when he looks up and sees her. He stops, pen poised above the credit card slip. She comes down the steps slowly, waiting for the Marine to follow. And Maya is waiting for him, alternately studying her reflection in the café window and the blue bauble on her wrist.

With a little help from Frankie's secretary, who seems to buy his story of the internship, it isn't hard to find Ingrid's address in the law school's records, and the day he gets it he springs into action. It's an apartment on Henderson, just south of the school, not far from where he lived back in the day. His plan is to drop by unannounced, an I-was-in-the-neighborhood thing. He considers calling, but it's too easy to say No on the phone, too hard to work his charms. He's changed his tactics slightly. She's one of the bright lights in the class, he'll tell her, and he's got a proposition. No, 'Opportunity' is the better word: he's got an opportunity for her. Frankie wouldn't approve, he's sure. But Frankie doesn't need to know.

He parks under a streetlight, sees the door to her unit. The light is on and he hesitates. He knows nothing about this girl other than that she's a knockout. If she's not living with the Marine, which she could be for all he knows, then there's probably a roommate. Roommates can be persuaded to make themselves scarce, though. Not a problem. He gazes at the soft glow through Ingrid's curtains. He sees shadowy movement and he's certain now of what he'll find. It's got to be the Marine.

The Marine gives him pause, an unfamiliar feeling of reluctance. The poor schmuck is a hero. A pawn, a sacrifice in a bloody mistake, but still a hero. He's given a piece of himself he'll never get back, and for what? That life was never something Lorenzo considered for himself. The service was for other guys, blockheads with a death wish, he used to think. And then there's this guy.

A hero, sure, but not Ingrid's type. That's clear. She deserves better. He can see that, the way she needs to be challenged, to be with her equal, not a charity case. She reminds him of his mother, in a way, a singer who could have made it big but, once she married his plodding father, never left town to pursue her dream. That was fine for her, she never complained, but this girl, Ingrid, surely she wants more. He pictures the two of them, back in Chicago, living the good life. He'll put the past in the past, everything forgotten. This bucolic interlude will be a fond memory for them both. They might bring his kids down to visit gramps, but otherwise, no, this place isn't for them. What was the name of that soldier boy you used to see? he'll ask, and she'll have to think hard before she pulls it back from some dim recess.

He steps to the door. Getting ahead of himself, he's already told Maya he can't see her again. She glanced at her new bracelet when he broke the news, as if he might want it back, but then relaxed when its significance sank in. He knows it could all be a mistake. He and Maya had a good run, they'd settled into a comfortable rhythm and Ingrid is a huge gamble. But then everything in life is a gamble. Time to move on. Looking for his niche, as he used to say.

He knocks. He should have brought flowers, he thinks. No. It's not a date. To make it seem real he should have brought files, a hint of the work she could expect on the job. He's surprised he's so unsure of himself, an unaccustomed state, he's surprised he broke it off with Maya prematurely, he's surprised he's standing in the dark outside this gorgeous stranger's apartment.

There is movement inside; he hears footsteps and a male voice. The Marine is with her after all. That's all right. The way it should be. Side by side. She can make a choice. There's no comparison. Hero or not, her future isn't with the Marine.

Light flashes in the peep-hole and he knows he's been seen. No turning back. The door edges open.

Ingrid stands in the shadowy entry, radiant. Her blond hair is pulled away from her flushed face. She's in a T-shirt, the school logo stretched full and punctuated by her nipples. Her feet are bare. She smiles with recognition.

"Mr. Rossi? What are you doing here?" She doesn't welcome him with open arms. She doesn't invite him in. She keeps the door open only a sliver. This isn't what he planned.

"Something I wanted to . . . discuss." His hand rises to the door, as if he might push his way in, although of course that's not what he intends. Still, he does want to see inside this girl's apartment more than he's wanted anything lately. He wants to be face to face with the Marine.

"No. I mean, now isn't . . . I'm . . . There's—"

"Let him in, Ingrid," comes a deep voice from inside the apartment.

The prospect of competing, of being demonstrably superior —defeating a rival at handball, on the battlefield, in the courtroom—arouses him. He breathes deeply, prepares for the challenge.

Ingrid pulls the door wide and he nearly tumbles in, steadies himself with the doorknob and follows her into the shadow, toward the voice.

The voice belongs to Frankie. He's sitting on the couch, a bottle of wine on the coffee table before him, two half-empty glasses. Frankie's feet are also bare, his dress shirt tieless and disheveled.

Frankie nods, eyes narrowed, his mouth twisted in a half-grin. "I told you this isn't Chicago, old buddy."

But Lorenzo is already backing toward the door as the truth explodes in him. He and Frankie, they're alike after all, too much alike. They always wanted the same things, just found different paths. And this is Frankie's backyard, his playground. Frankie can't let him win here. He should have seen that, should have understood that this isn't for him, this town, this life. Like wings on a pig, Frankie would say.

"Lorenzo," Frankie whispers, not unkindly, hoisting a glass.

He backs further away, leaving Frankie and Ingrid in shadow. He doesn't want to hear what Frankie has to say. He knows now what he should have known long ago. He's dead weight. His father doesn't need him. Frankie doesn't. And he's been on the wrong road for far too long. He should be anywhere but here. He doesn't belong here. He doesn't belong.

SOPHIE, SOPHIA

I close the laptop as Lynn enters the kitchen, casually, so as not to suggest I'm hiding anything. I'm not hiding anything, in fact. The screen has been blank for at least a minute and I consider, briefly, reopening the laptop so she will see this. But it's too late to make a point, and she'll think whatever she thinks.

Lynn looks nice this morning. When I got up an hour ago, trying not to wake her but knowing that the running shower would, her graying hair was a mess, crushed against the pillow, her face splotchy with sleep. Now the color in her cheeks is restored; her hair is washed and buoyant. She's wearing a bulky sweater, one that hides the weight she's gained these past few years, but it's attractive: blue with silver threads running through it and a scoop neck that reveals a crisp, white blouse. She doesn't always wear makeup on Saturdays, but today she even has a touch of eye shadow. And is that lilac I smell?

"What's on tap for today?" she asks, pouring coffee from the pot I made, strong, the way she likes it.

"Work," I say and nod at the computer as if that explains everything.

I don't think she knows what I've been doing. It's all innocent enough, really, but one night a month or so ago she nearly caught me. I'd been watching streaming video, a grainy shot of this girl Sophie in bed with an older man. That particular site specializes in guys my age getting it on with nubile, big-breasted teens, and that's the point, the fantasy of it. If that old bastard, with the non-existent hairline and the flab and the droopy balls, can be with a hard-bodied young thing in a cheerleader outfit, or a candy striper's uniform, then so can I. When Lynn walked in on me that day, Sophie and the old guy had just finished and I was thinking about where I could be alone for a few minutes, and believe me that's all I was thinking about. She might have seen the screen before I could gather my wits and close it that time, and she studied me long and hard. My face burned. But she didn't say anything. She turned around and left the room, and after that I was more careful.

"I was thinking we'd rent a movie tonight," she says now. "Order in?"

"Sure," I say. "Pick whatever you want."

I've been married to Lynn for twenty-eight years, since right after college. Our sex life has never been what I'd call satisfying. Even when we were younger she didn't seem to enjoy it. We had a child, a boy, after we'd been married a couple of years. He was stillborn. His name was Gordon, like me. After that, she let me do what I had to do, with no encouragement, no effort on her part, but I think she was afraid of what might happen if she got pregnant again. I understood. She couldn't face it. Eventually, I took the hint and gave up. We didn't talk about it and we didn't move to separate beds. I never considered leaving her. How could I? We just stopped touching each other.

In the '80s I had an affair with a woman in my office, a claims adjuster, Roberta. It wasn't something I sought, it just happened, or Roberta made it happen, and half the time I felt alive and wonderful and the rest of the time I felt lousy, for lying to Lynn, for breaking promises. After a couple of months, I ended it and I don't plan to repeat it, even if another Roberta comes along. I'm not a disloyal person. I know about loss. But, here's the thing, I'm a man. I have needs, you might say, and they don't go away. Mostly I've been content to steal moments with hidden magazines or, on business trips, the occasional movie on an adult cable channel in the hotel. Sometimes I wished it were otherwise, that I could experience the warmth of a woman's touch. But it was enough.

Until recently. A few months ago I found out what was available on the Internet. No magazines to hide, no worry about what charges show up on a hotel bill that Lynn might see.

I've always known there were places on the web where you could look at girls, of course. Guys at work talk about such things. I suppose I've even read about it in the newspaper, articles instructing parents how to keep children innocent a day or two longer, but I'd never thought to hunt for them. And then one day I was searching on the computer for something else—a particular kind of squirrel-resistant birdfeeder Lynn wanted, I think—and somehow I came across a picture of a girl called Sophie. Petite, glossy brown hair. Large breasts, but not too large. Tiny tan lines. A lusty, young look, healthy, fresh, with nothing like tattoos or piercings or anything else that said porn star. It turned out to be a series of pictures, beginning with her fully clothed, wearing dark-rimmed glasses and a pin-stripe suit, taking dictation from a gray-bearded man in an office. By the end, she was naked and the old guy was kissing her. To see more, the website touted, all you needed was a credit card.

I know it's trite, but I couldn't stop thinking about her. She was perfect, more like a painting than a real girl. Later, while Lynn was out at the grocery store, I lay on the couch in the basement in the dark, slipped my pants down and . . . imagined her. I was the boss behind the desk, Sophie worked for me and was happy to do my bidding.

When I went back to that website, the free images, the teasers, weren't enough. I needed more explicit fuel for the fantasy. Access to the site for one month was $29.95 billed to a credit card. Lynn would wonder what the charge was for, but the site promised an ambiguous reference, the equivalent of a brown-paper wrapper, and in any case I would intercept the bill. She wouldn't have to see it and even if she did and guessed what it was I'd say it was a mistake, that I'd get it straightened out. And so I paid, and watched as Sophie and the old man made love on the desk. In the chair. On the floor. Hers was the most perfect body I had ever seen, her lovemaking natural and genuine.

I needed still more. The next time I was alone I looked for other sites, similarly themed. Older man, younger woman.

And there she was again, the same girl, unmistakable, but this time her name was Sophia. Her hair, that lustrous brown, was now up, exposing more of her face and tender neck. The image was sharper and her smooth, young skin glowed. Her green eyes stared straight into the camera; she whispered directly to me. I paid another $29.95 to watch her with a different old man, in the back seat of a limousine. She was sweet, innocent, hungry.

That website sold DVDs of Sophia, one by herself, one with the old man. I ordered them both, had them sent to the office, plotting how I would keep them from Jean, my secretary. For days I managed to grab the mail before she did, behavior I'm sure Jean found odd. When they finally arrived I was breathless, anxious to see Sophia, to be even closer to her. At work, after closing the door, I went online, aware that there was a chance my browsing would not go unnoticed, and watched the streaming video of Sophie as a secretary, then Sophia in the limo. I searched and found another clip of Sophie, this time with a young guy, a muscular redhead who made me think of my son, who never lived, who never felt, and I couldn't watch.

Now Lynn is out and I've taken the laptop into the study. Since their arrival, I've watched both DVDs a dozen times, whenever I'm in the house alone. I keep them in my briefcase, where Lynn would never look. And I return to the website almost daily to see Sophie, to be with Sophia. It occurs to me that my fantasy is complex. It is not that I simply picture being with her, giving her pleasure and receiving the same from her. That's pornography, the uncontrollable impulses of an adolescent. My fantasy is that I know her, I have a relationship with her that transcends sex. I speak to her on the telephone. I write love notes when we're apart. We will be together forever, Sophie and I. She is far more of a distraction, far more real to me, than my brief affair with Roberta years ago. More real, it shocks me to see, than my love for Lynn.

But it isn't enough. I need more. If there is a Sophie and a Sophia, I reason, might there not also be a Sally, a Sarah? Might there be a way to meet her? I go onto the Internet and search for Sophie, Sophia. It takes only a few sites to find what I'm looking for. An exotic dancer under the stage name Sophie, she dances at clubs around the country and she's done porn as Sophia, Samantha, Shilo. There are more sites, more names.

But her *real* name is Sandra Kaminsky.

And she's dead.

Lynn is back. I hear her in the kitchen so I shut down the computer. My palms are sweating, heart pounding like a lovesick teenager. Such a cliché! Sophie is dead, a young life extinguished, and suddenly all the air is gone. I can't breathe, I can't swallow. How can this lovely, healthy girl be dead, gone when we've only just met?

For dinner Lynn orders pizza, something we haven't done in years. When the Domino's kid is at the door and I'm fishing in my wallet, I realize he must be the same age as Sophie and I know it's irrational—I don't even know yet where she lived, it could be anywhere—but I wonder if they knew each other. In my mind I'm certain they did. I want to think of her having a life like this, flesh and blood, alive. I want to tell him that I know Sophie is dead, that it's a tragedy and I'm sorry for his loss.

"Here's to the weekend," Lynn says, clinking her wine glass against mine. She has opened a nice Bordeaux, too good for pizza but a vintage she likes, one that has aged well.

"Makes it all worthwhile," I say.

Spices in the pepperoni bite my tongue, the wine at first soothes and then unsettles as it makes me think of what will never be. Gordon, Sophie. Lynn has lit candles. She sits close at the dining table, the lilacs strong. I can feel her watching.

When Lynn is asleep, I slip out of bed and go back to the computer, wincing at the whirring noise it makes, as loud as a jet engine when the rest of the night is so silent, and look again for Sophie. Sophia. Sandra.

There's an article from a newspaper. She was murdered. Over a year ago, in Canada, where she'd been working in a strip club. She'd gone missing. Her family, from Cleveland, went to look for her. Her mother denied that her daughter did porn. Working her way through college as a dancer, she said. After two weeks the body was found in an abandoned quarry, strangled, raped. There was a picture of her as a young girl in glasses, smiling.

As if hidden by a passing cloud, the light from the hall suddenly dims, and I see Lynn in the doorway. She wears a bathrobe but is standing in shadow and that's all I can see. For a moment I imagine that it's Sophie standing there, young Sophie who is dead, who's been dead for as long as I've known her, for as long as she's been coming to my bed, for as long as our improbable romance has kept me alive.

"Who is she," Lynn says.

"What?"

"You're seeing someone and I want to know who she is."

So this is what she suspects. I'm almost relieved. "Don't be ridiculous," I say. "I can't sleep, is all."

"The sneaking around, the emails or whatever. Do you think I can't read you? After all these years?"

"I don't know what you're talking about."

Now she comes into the room. The screen of the laptop is up, a picture of Sophie, nude, gazing out at me. Vibrant, alive. I make no attempt to hide it. If she takes three more steps, two, she'll see. I think I even want her to see, so I can tell her about this poor girl.

"It doesn't matter, you know," she says and takes another step. "I don't blame you."

"You're talking nonsense, Lynnie. That's all in the past. There's no one."

"Because I know I haven't—"

"Hush."

She takes one more step and I now imagine she can see Sophie, if not the picture on the screen then the girl's reflection in my eyes, and I wonder what my wife is thinking. There is the scent of lilacs between us again and I realize Lynn has brushed her hair. She does look lovely in the dim light of my den. She's been a good wife.

I shut the computer off and close the screen.

"Come to bed," she says.

AMERICAN MARSUPIAL

Danny Fleischman's keys slipped from his sweat-slicked fingers and fell to the brownstone's stoop. As he bent to retrieve them, he felt his heart race, like a CD on fast forward, bass thumping double-time in his chest. His hands shook. On the third try, he managed to plunge the key into the lock.

He found Andrea in their narrow kitchen, chopping tomatoes in the Cuisinart, watching on their portable Samsung CNN's perpetual replay of the Monument falling, like a cartoon tree—all 555 feet of it, landing every time with a thud that seemed to shake the video camera of the lucky tourist who captured the catastrophe, accompanied by a chorus of gasps and screams and a rolling cloud of dust. Danny deposited his briefcase on the counter. He felt the sensation of dust on his tongue, unclipped the cellphone from his belt, lifted his wife's skirt, and climbed into her womb.

His pulse slowed, the beating of his heart quieted in the close, dark space. He felt the warmth of the womb surround him.

While the news loop continued on TV, Andrea grunted and pushed and dragged him out.

"I don't have time for this, Danny," she said. He squinted and blinked, the world's bright lights stinging his eyes, and lifted a foot to climb back in. Little Jeremy got there first.

"Me," said the boy.

Danny treasured his son. He remembered the painful delivery, when no one noticed that his own convulsions matched Andrea's. He marveled every day that this growing, learning creature had come from him, and now was becoming part of the universe, whether they liked it or not. And of course, Jeremy needed his mother. It was understandable. But everyone seemed to forget that he had needs, too.

"Me," said Danny. He tugged and struggled with his son until Andrea shoved him away and let Jeremy in.

"Jeremy is the child, Danny. It's his right."

"But I was here first," he whined. He took a beer from the stainless Kenmore, slammed the door, winced guiltily at the whoosh of air, the clank of bottles inside, and stomped into the living room.

Earlier, at work, in the glass and steel Miracle Mile skyscraper where for seven years he'd toiled as a copywriter, news of the attack had spread fast, leaping virally from cubicle to cubicle: there was an explosion on the Mall in Washington. Not a hijacked plane this time—a bomb. Danny's vacationing boss kept a TV in her office, a flat-screen Panasonic, and the hushed staff crowded around. All the Chicago stations showed the same thing. The Monument fell. The Monument fell. The Monument fell again.

"We should evacuate," Danny had said, looking from Mindy, another copywriter, to Gerald, to the guy from Accounting, back to Mindy. His voice trembled and caught. "Don't you think we should evacuate?"

In the absence of their boss, who was with her husband on a Mexican beach, Danny was in charge. No one had ever said as much, since the boss expected to be called on her cell for anything important, but to Danny it was self-evident. Sure, there were others with more seniority, but he'd been there a long time—going on seven years—and was tall and good looking, unquestionably the boss's favorite. She'd expect him to lead the troops in a crisis.

"Shouldn't we?" he asked.

Mindy rolled her eyes. "It's in *Washington*," she said. "*We're* in *Chicago*."

Mindy had grown up in the south suburbs and pronounced "Washington" and "Chicago" with a nasal twang that tickled Danny's north suburban ears. His mother was a Southsider. He loved listening to Mindy talk.

Andrea, on the other hand, his wife of five years, was from Massachusetts. They'd met when Danny was in Boston for his one-semester stab at law school, abandoned after an intense Socratic grilling by the Contracts prof that left Danny lightheaded, and short of breath, and longing for Chicago. When he saw her in a coffee shop, sipping a latte, foam icing her lip, he'd felt an instant attraction. He struck up a conversation. Her accent was all wrong, her r's twisted like backwards underwear. But she was freckled and short and had an upturned nose. Like his mother.

His mother, who got him a shot at his job—she knew someone who knew someone—despite no advertising qualifications, no experience of any kind. His mother, who pressed his shirt for the interview, knotted his tie, shined his shoes. That was the day he met Mindy.

Before he and Andrea were married, and before Andrea had moved out to Chicago from her beloved, ancestral Boston to be with him, but after they'd been engaged long-distance for more than two years, and with the wedding closing in on him like an asteroid racing calamitously toward Earth, Danny and Mindy had an affair. It was torrid. Mindy had skills. He broke it off a week before the ceremony.

The Monument fell, and fell.

He always knew there'd be heart problems, on top of everything else. Hadn't his mother's uncle died of a heart attack? Uncle Chet was seventy-something, of course, but that didn't mean Danny would be immune, even as a young man, no matter what the EKG said. He first became aware of the chest pains following that disastrous half-year in law school, after he'd met Andrea, become engaged, dropped out and moved back home, after he'd lucked into the ad agency job, after he'd started seeing Mindy on the side. He saw a doctor. And when that doctor was no help, he saw another. And another.

After his latest visit to this latest doctor, Danny decided not to go back to the office. Why should he? He'd made it clear enough to anyone who was listening—and he knew Mindy heard everything, it was what made her both an outstanding copywriter and, in those distant days, an attentive, scrupulous lover—that he wasn't feeling well, that his fingers tingled and he couldn't catch his breath, that the doctor would squeeze him in. Never mind that this Dr. Shapiro could find nothing wrong. He was a quack, they were all quacks. Danny had a weak heart, it was obvious, it was why he'd quit his regular tennis matches with Marc Silverblatt, it was why he'd had to stop going to the gym and avoid climbing stairs and shoveling snow, and if something happened to him, if his heart exploded in his chest as Danny knew one day it would, leaving Andrea alone and Jeremy without a father, depriving his mother of her only son, then Shapiro and all the other so-called doctors would have hell to pay.

And besides, he couldn't get the image of the Monument out of his mind, falling over and over again. It was bad enough that even days later there was hardly anything else on TV. But the collapse now was in his head, etched there, indelible. They had struck at the symbol of America's might and deflated the national conscience. And he wasn't feeling too well himself.

He went home. Not his home, where he lived with Andrea and Jeremy, but *home* home, the house in Winnetka where he grew up. When he came back from Boston, he'd lived in the apartment above his parents' garage, and he drove every day down Sheridan Road and along Lake Shore Drive to Michigan Avenue, certain that the tumor growing inside his left temporal lobe, that the CT scans never seemed to find, would finally reach the point at which his vision blurred and he would miss the S turn at Diversey, plunging into the Lincoln Park lagoon.

He parked in the driveway. Instead of heading directly into the house, he moved to the steep steps leading up to his old apartment. Those were carefree days, except for his health. No child to compete with, no responsibilities, no falling Monuments. A wonderful life. He started up the steps, clutched his chest, felt the sweat bead on his forehead, and lifted one foot after the other. Inside, in the lemony air his mother kept fresh for him, he collapsed on the sofa. He closed his eyes. He imagined the embracing aroma of baking bread. The door creaked open.

"I saw your car in the driveway, dear." His mother came in, bearing a tray. "Tell me about your day."

Although she spoke like Mindy and resembled Andrea, his mother had swollen over the years, in her bosom, her hips. He eyed her ampleness, watched her float across the room like a billowy cloud.

She set the tray on the coffee table, turned the plate of chocolate chip cookies so that the largest was within Danny's reach, and pushed the tall glass of milk toward him.

"I wasn't feeling well, Mom."

"We're having spaghetti and meatballs for dinner. Your favorite!"

His mother drifted next to him, spread her legs and let him climb inside. He felt her beating heart, surrendered himself to the warmth of her.

"Andrea doesn't understand me." Danny stared at the ceiling over his bed in the Marriott "She's changed."

"She's never been right for you," said Mindy, raising one arm, stroking Danny's shoulder with the other.

They'd flown out to San Francisco together for the American Advertising Association convention. On the plane, Danny drank three whiskey sours—he told Mindy over and over how much he hated flying, while she stroked his arm and cooed—and at the hotel they wound up in the bar, then his room.

"It's always 'Jeremy this' and 'Jeremy that.' She used to have time for me."

Mindy kissed Danny's cheek. "I've got time."

Danny curled against her, felt her warmth, her dampness. He closed his eyes and wondered if she could give him what he needed, wondered if there was room enough inside.

"You work too hard," she said. "You need someone who can take care of you. I waited. I knew you'd come around."

"You went to the doctor again? What's that—the third time this week?" Andrea served a bowl of mac and cheese to Jeremy, then poured marinara sauce on Danny's spaghetti and cut him a thick slice of garlic bread.

It was the fifth time, actually. He hadn't told her about the Wednesday visits, one before work and one after lunch, when he was sure his heart was preparing to quit.

"We talked about this, Danny. You've got to see someone about this obsession."

"Are there meatballs?" he asked.

Andrea clucked and shook her head.

He couldn't tune out the droning television, the little Samsung in the kitchen, the Zenith in the living room, the sound of the Monument falling again and again, the shrieks. It had been more than a month and still it was all over the news, like a new theme song for life in America. He was sick of hearing about it, America under attack, the knife in America's heart. Al Qaeda had claimed responsibility, but so had the Aryan Brotherhood and a previously unknown kook who demanded freedom for the Unabomber. It didn't matter who did it. America was afraid.

"It's hardly my fault that I'm sick." He reached for her skirt.

She slapped his hand away. "I think we both know whose fault it is."

He looked at his wife. He blinked. How could he ever have thought she looked like his mother? They weren't at all alike. With his fingers, he picked a noodle from his plate, put it in his mouth, and sucked it all the way in. Jeremy applauded and laughed.

"Danny," Andrea said, her face contorted in a reproving frown.

Again he reached for her and slowly sank to his knees. He lifted her skirt.

He drove up to Winnetka. He'd told Andrea he had to work on Sunday, and he'd told Mindy that Andrea had demanded he take her and Jeremy to see the dinosaurs at the Natural History Museum. After the San Francisco trip, he'd been seeing Mindy regularly: long lunches, spent at her place in Sandburg Village; nights, when he told Andrea he had to work late; a trip to New York for another conference, one that didn't exist. Exhausted, Danny slipped into his parents' house.

His mother was cooking a corned beef while slicing and chopping cabbage for slaw. She raised her cheek to be kissed. He took a beer from the refrigerator and joined his father on the couch in the living room, watching the Magnavox big screen. The Monument fell.

"Dad, can't we watch something else? A ball game? A movie?"

"It's the world, son. It's news. It's what's important." The Monument fell.

Danny headed out to the garage apartment. His mother hadn't changed a thing since he lived there, just as she'd left his room in the house untouched from his high school days, with his trophies and that Pearl Jam poster. In the apartment were his old boombox, a tower of cassette tapes, a mini fridge that his mother kept stocked with Miller Lite, a 2001 calendar tacked to the wall. September was circled, the month he got married, the month the world changed, the month time stood still. He lay on the bed, closed his eyes.

When he woke, Mindy stood over him. Her arms were crossed, lips pursed.

"The museum, huh? Dinosaurs?"

He blinked, tried to make the dream go away. She wasn't a dream.

"I went there," she said. "I wanted to watch you with your kid. To see your wife. I looked all over the fucking museum."

"It was . . ." No, she knew it wasn't closed. "He . . . changed his mind, wanted to go to the park."

"I called your house. Your wife answered."

"She—"

"I drove by. Looked in the window. They were both inside."

The door swung open and Danny's mother appeared, wearing an apron, a steaming plate of beef and boiled potatoes balanced on her hand. "Oh," she said, stopping in the open door, and then, "Oh," again.

"Tell him to come down here to eat, for cryin' out loud," came the voice of his father, shouted from the kitchen window.

"Grandma!" That was Jeremy's voice, followed by the slammed door to Andrea's minivan and then *her* voice. "Is he here?"

"Oh," said his mother, nearly dropping the overloaded plate.

Jeremy's footsteps on the stairs, followed by Andrea's, then his father's.

Andrea glared at Mindy from the door. Mindy glared back. The Monument fell.

"We meet at last," said Mindy. Now her familiar accent made him wince.

"Are you sleeping?" asked Jeremy and jumped onto the bed, still clutching his Gameboy. Danny wondered what he could ever teach this child, who would grow up in a world that wasn't safe, where there was nowhere to hide.

"Who is she?" asked Andrea, still looking at Mindy.

"On the news," said his father. "They're saying it wasn't Al Qaeda. It was some anti-war whackos. I knew it all along. Makes you think, doesn't it?"

"What's going on?" asked his mother.

"I mean, who can you trust?" asked his father.

"She's not right for you," said Mindy. "You said so yourself."

"*This* is who you've been sleeping with?" Andrea was nearly shouting. "Her?"

"Oh, my," said his mother.

"I—" began Danny.

"Daddy?" said Jeremy. How could he protect his son? It was a dangerous world.

"Danny," said Mindy and Andrea, and his mother.

"Son?" said his father.

Danny looked at his son, then at Mindy and Andrea, his parents. He closed his eyes and saw the Monument falling, the rolling cloud of dust. He heard the shrieks and sirens. It could happen here, it could happen anywhere. No one was safe. No one. He curled tight on the bed, burying his face beneath the pillow, pulled the blanket over him. He felt the warmth of his own blood, heard the pulsing beat of his own heart, and willed them all to be gone.

PLUCK

My return to teaching was reluctant, to say the least. Based on the enthusiasm I'd felt from my agent and my editor, I'd had high hopes that my last book would free me from academic drudgery. There was the healthy advance I received, the largest of my career, and even before the book was published we sold a film option. All signs pointed to a bestseller, if not a blockbuster, and my effort to use highbrow literary technique to write a thriller was, it seemed, looking smart. The publisher had a right of first refusal on my next book, which I'd already started. I had an extensive tour planned, a dozen or more cities, readings, radio interviews, the whole works. The future, as they say, was looking bright.

But we all know what they also say about counting your chickens.

First, there was the divorce. The end of my marriage was not, to be fair, completely unexpected. Beth and I had been drifting apart for years, the pace of that drift accelerating when our children left for college. What *was* a surprise, though, was the sudden cataclysm that split our union irrevocably: the revelation that Beth had for years been carrying on an affair with her dentist. Her dentist! And while I felt that I was obviously the injured party in the proceedings, my advance, which I'd planned to live on as I wrote the new book, evaporated in a cloud of lawyers' fees and the divorce settlement. Then the publisher got cold feet, hearing rumors—rumors that originated with my ex-wife, I'd wager—that a plagiarism claim was in the offing.

I made it clear to my agent that this was impossible, that the novel was completely the work of my imagination, but nothing I could say would revive the publisher's former enthusiasm. Support for the tour vanished. Advertising never materialized. The film option expired. And the book, with absolutely no fanfare, was dead on arrival. I managed an appearance at the local Barnes & Noble and an indie bookstore in a Chicago suburb near my former home, and that was pretty much it.

All of which meant that I was suddenly in need of a source of income, like almost every fiction writer in the country. I called old friends and considered myself extremely fortunate when one of them helped me land a visiting writer gig at Indiana University, a fine institution with a storied creative writing program. It was an appointment for a single academic year, but I figured I'd either convince the department to renew the appointment or I'd come up with something permanent while I finished my new book and continued to put the disaster of my marriage behind me. I packed my belongings—what little my wife allowed me to keep—and moved into a one-bedroom apartment in Bloomington to start over. It wasn't what I wanted to be doing at that point in my career, but thanks to Beth and her dentist my options were limited.

Not that I disliked the students or even the time spent in the classroom. I found it invigorating. And I worked hard. I gave my classes my full attention. I was respectful to male and female students alike. I created a safe, supportive environment, especially in the workshops, where I would not tolerate the kind of personal attacks I'd experienced myself in graduate school. I made decent progress on my new novel. My students seemed to like working with me. My evaluations were, for the most part, glowing.

So, all in all, life was OK. Not great. I'd hit bottom, but maybe I was beginning the climb back. The semester took a lot out of me and I was looking forward to the Christmas break to rest, to get some writing done, and generally to decompress. My kids were going to spend the holidays with their mother in Chicago, and I expected to miss them, but we'd talked about a spring visit, and that was OK, too, for now.

I'm not sure what it is about single people, especially the recently divorced, but one of my new friends on the faculty invited me to join her and her husband for Christmas dinner at their home. Couples assume singles must be terribly lonely at the holidays, and I suppose some are. But I truly was looking forward to the time by myself to work on my novel. When Charlotte called, though, and said that she and Jackson were having a few people over, people also from the writing and publishing world, and she was sure I'd find them interesting, I didn't refuse. Even though I really did not want to go, even more than that I didn't want to seem pathetic, and Charlotte and her husband are very nice people whom I did not want to offend. So I accepted. And then immediately regretted it. It might snow, I told myself, or I might come down with a cold, or some other excuse would present itself, and the dinner would be avoided. Somehow.

The day came, and it didn't snow. I felt fine. Better than fine. Christmas morning dawned bright and sunny, if cold. Bloomington is a lovely town, as I'd discovered in my explorations throughout the fall, and the university's campus is one of the most beautiful anywhere. When it's depopulated, though, when there are no students walking the wooded campus pathways, it takes on a different appearance. It's still beautiful, but more as a work of art than a living, breathing experience. Deciding to take a Christmas Day walk, I struck out from my little apartment, bundled with hat and scarf, and launched into the windy, deserted campus.

Walking is my favorite way of resolving problems on the page in a work in progress. It's a meditative act, a time to let the subconscious take over and draw out solutions I would never come to while sitting at my desk staring at the computer screen. Sometimes the problems are resolved by addressing questions I didn't know I had. Given my personal situation, it should come as no surprise that my current manuscript is about a marriage that has fallen apart. Naturally, I'd been writing it from the point of view of the husband, which is the story I understand best, but I was too close to that angle, and the narrative wasn't coming alive. As I strolled through the heart of the deserted campus, I wondered what would happen if I looked at it differently. Not from the wife's point of view, of course, but what about the kids? What if I alternated between the points of view of the son and daughter of the couple breaking up? That idea got me excited and I picked up my pace so I could complete my circuit of the campus to get back to my laptop and jot down some ideas.

My cell phone rang just as I passed the library, a brutalist behemoth that looked particularly forlorn and deserted in the cold. I dared to hope that it was Charlotte, canceling the dinner. Maybe Jackson was ill, or the power was out, or she hadn't been able to find the right ingredients for the tofurkey. But, no, the screen warned that the caller was Beth. My immediate impulse was to decline the call, or ignore it, even though it might have been about the kids, or giving the kids an opportunity to wish me a Merry Christmas, or something equally benign. Which would have been sweet, but what I really wanted more than anything was to get to my desk and work. It was in any case more likely that she was calling with some harangue about money or a perceived slight of one sort or another. So I didn't take the call. Let her leave a message. If it's the kids, that's probably easier for them, too. We'll all be happier without another awkward phone conversation.

I love my kids. I admit that I haven't been the best father in the world, although let's keep in mind that the divorce happened because their mother had an affair with her dentist, not because I heaped abuse on them or her. Still, as an obsessive writer, I was probably absent from their childhood more than fathers who had normal jobs. I was traveling for research or book promotion, or I was tucked away in my studio, the door locked to prevent the very sort of distractions that children are prone to cause. And my wife, for all her faults—the dentist, of all people!—did manage most of the time to protect my writing isolation, either keeping the kids occupied with toys and games or trips to the park when they were younger, or chauffeuring them to their various after-school activities as they grew. Or at least that's what she told me later when I asked what they'd been up to. I always wondered what I might learn about my wife if I grilled the kids. Where did they *really* go while I was working?

I listened to Beth's message, which, to my surprise, was an unexpectedly nice holiday greeting, not her usual jeremiad. I almost wished I'd taken her call, although I knew from experience that even otherwise friendly exchanges with her had a tendency to devolve into bitterness, so it was just as well that I hadn't. In the Christmas spirit, I'd shoot her an email greeting later, and we both could congratulate ourselves for being civil.

From campus I hurried back to my apartment, made strong coffee, and started a rewrite of my opening chapter from the point of view of the daughter, already thinking of how the angle would change when I switched to the son's point of view for chapter two. The words streamed out of me faster than ever, sentences practically writing themselves. It's a dangerous feeling, but I liked the work I'd done and I lost track of time. Eventually I noticed that the light in the room had altered and I looked at my watch. I would be late for dinner. There was no time to change, no time for anything. I grabbed a bottle of wine from my cupboard, hoped it would pair adequately with the vegetarian feast, whatever it turned out to be, and ran out the door.

I headed east from Bloomington into the hills of Brown County, where Charlotte and Jackson lived near the touristy town of Nashville, about thirty minutes from campus. Leaving the main highway, I followed a winding road south along the edge of the state park that was one of the area's main attractions. I had never been to Charlotte's house, so I wasn't sure of the way, despite her detailed directions and the guidance of the GPS on my phone. It was now late afternoon and the sun had already disappeared behind the towering pines that lined the road, deepening my anxiety that I had misread the directions and had lost my way. Eventually, though, I spotted the gravel drive I'd been told to expect, and turned into their yard, which had been carved from the forest to embrace a sprawling cedar-clad split level.

As I climbed out of my car, Jackson emerged to usher me into the house. Unlike my diminished state and minimalist quarters, Charlotte's home was expansive and lovely, filled with rustic furnishings—bookshelves made from weathered wood, an antique sideboard, a milk can repurposed as an end table. Their dining table was set for four, a smaller number than I'd envisioned, but now I was curious about the only other guest. I even briefly wondered if Charlotte had expected me to bring a date, but I could recall no discussion to that effect, and couldn't imagine who she thought I might invite. She had certainly mentioned people I should meet. Had that changed?

Jackson lifted a bottle of Scotch from his bar in an offering gesture and I nodded. He poured two fingers into a glass and poured another for himself. He raised his glass in salute and took a sip.

"Charlotte will be down in a minute," he said apologetically. Jackson was an interesting fellow with whom I'd had only passing interactions. An artisan, Charlotte had told me, who did his work in their barn and sold his wares through a gallery in Nashville. I wondered if the shelves and the milk can were his creations. Charlotte, though, had a PhD in medieval studies and they made an unlikely pair. But maybe that's what it took to build a sturdy relationship. Maybe my marriage failed because Beth, another writer, and I were too much alike. Probably she and her dentist would last, then, although I couldn't imagine it.

"It's not as cold as it was yesterday," I said, struggling for conversation.

"Still brisk out there," Jackson said.

"Indeed," I said.

Thankfully, Charlotte appeared and we embraced. "Merry Christmas," she said. Not that I was expecting Christmas attire, but I was somewhat taken aback to see her wearing somber gray slacks and a black sweater. It suited her, but was hardly festive.

"Same to you," I said.

"He brought wine," Jackson said, nodding to the bottle we'd deposited on the bar.

"Wonderful," she said, reaching for the Scotch. She wasn't the kind of woman to wait for her husband to make her a drink. Unlike Beth.

Charlotte busied herself in the kitchen, where Jackson and I dutifully followed to watch her chop veggies, slice cheese, arrange crackers on a plate. Nothing was said of our other dinner companion, which puzzled me no end. I'd arrived a good half hour after the time Charlotte had indicated. Who was this mystery guest, and where was he? Or she?

Finally Charlotte was done with preparations for dinner, which was apparently already cooking in various pots and ovens. She lifted the platter of hors d'oeuvres and led the way into the living room where Jackson rebuilt the fire and Charlotte refreshed our drinks. As soon as we had settled, we were alerted by the sound of tires on gravel to the arrival of the other guest for dinner. Charlotte rose and waited by the door, welcoming the newcomer with a broad embrace before pulling him inside out of the cold where I finally saw his face. Angus Denholm, that old son-of-a-bitch.

I rose, but wondered if he would shake my hand if I extended it.

"Angus," I said.

He hesitated. Was it possible that he didn't recognize me? Charlotte apparently didn't know that there was a time Angus would rather slug me than be in the same room. That was a long time ago, though, at Iowa, when we competed for everything—women, fellowships, the praise of our fiction workshop teachers. He never forgave me for marrying Beth, the prettiest writer in the program. Did he know about the dentist?

"Dick," Angus said, nodding in my direction.

"Ah," Charlotte said. "I guess introductions are unnecessary."

"Yes," I said, wondering if I should take my bottle of wine and head home.

"Two novelists," she said. "It really is a small world." Her earlier holiday cheer had deflated as she detected the tension between us. It did not bode well for a small dinner party. She looked at me with some frustration, as if asking why I hadn't told her. But how could I know who her other guest was? She never mentioned a name. And what the hell was he doing in Indiana anyway?

Angus Denholm's first novel came out when he was still in his twenties, shortly after we left Iowa, and announced his arrival on the literary scene in a big way. While many writers fade with their second effort, Angus earned even more attention with a collection of short stories that was, improbably, a finalist for the National Book Award, after which, I was told, he became insufferable. In all the time Beth and I were married, we talked about him only once, when he eventually won the Pulitzer for a slim volume that was more character study than novel, although I suspected from the reverential tone in that conversation that she had followed his career more closely than I.

Jackson poured another round. That was one way to deal with the situation, I thought. If we all got stinking drunk, we'd either come to blows or pass out. Better than burning silence, whichever the outcome. I didn't know or care much where Angus lived, but I was prepared to sleep it off in my car, if I had to. I gladly accepted the drink.

Not a moment too soon, Charlotte announced that dinner was ready. We found our places, with Jackson at one end, Charlotte at the other, and Angus and I facing each other on the sides.

"So, Dick," Angus said, "what are you working on?"

That was most definitely not a conversation I wanted to have with him. I'm sufficiently self-aware to realize that part of my present antagonism toward Angus Denholm is the result of jealousy. His publishing star has far outshone mine. But long before we'd published our first books, I hated the guy. He just rubbed me the wrong way.

"A new novel," I said. "You?" Not that I gave a rat's ass.

"Final edits," he said. "Fitzsimmons at Random House has been great to work with. This is our fourth—no, fifth—book together."

Fuck you, Angus.

Charlotte served the nut loaf, which collapsed into a fragrant, steaming mess on the plate. Jackson passed the mashed potatoes. Angus hoarded the gravy. I drank my Scotch.

Our hosts did their best to keep the conversation alive. Jackson was a basketball fan and expressed his expectations for a stellar season for the Hoosiers after several mediocre years. Charlotte observed that the music school had an amazing concert series planned for the coming months featuring world-class visiting faculty.

"Remember Pluck?" Angus asked me suddenly.

I had no idea who Pluck was.

"Who's Pluck?" Charlotte asked. "And what an odd name."

"Funny story about that," Angus said, directing his comment at me. "It was actually Dick's wife who gave him the name."

It was coming back to me now. The dog.

"I was sharing an old farmhouse with a couple of other grad students. You remember Jake Morgan and Lance Shuler, don't you Dick? Terrible place, that house. I don't think it had been condemned, but it surely was close, although after a while you didn't even notice the crumbling, mildewed walls or the skittering of mice in the dark. Anyway, one day I came back to the house after workshop feeling like shit, and there was this dog sitting on our front porch like he owned the place. Mangy old thing, tongue hanging out of its mouth, ribs showing. I went toward the door and damned if the dog didn't growl and bare its teeth, like it was a goddamn guard dog.

"Since I wasn't getting in through the front door, I went around back to the kitchen door. When I looked out front, I saw that the dog was still there. I felt sorry for him, like maybe he belonged to the people who used to live in this dump—long gone as I understood it—and he'd come back to find them. I looked around the kitchen for something I could feed the mutt. There wasn't much, but we did have some overripe bananas that Lance had picked up somewhere and probably wouldn't miss. I grabbed a couple of those and opened the front door.

"Now that I was on the inside and no longer an intruder, the pooch looked at me expectantly. I peeled one of the bananas and fed it to him. I suppose he would have eaten just about anything, but he snarfed both of those bananas in record time and looked up at me for more.

I went back to the kitchen. There was a white carton of rice leftover from last week's Chinese takeout, so I gave him that and he used that long tongue of his to lap up every last grain of it. Jake had some Cheerios, so I gave the dog a bowl of that—no milk in the house, but I figured he wouldn't care. Gone in a flash. I filled the bowl with water. He drank that.

"I said to him, 'That's it buddy, there's not one more morsel of food in this house.'" He looked around me into the house, like he was checking to see if I was telling the truth, then licked my hand and trotted off, headed who knows where. Gone for good, I figured.

"That weekend we were hosting a bash at the house, with a keg and bonfire and the whole deal. Just about everyone was going to be there. Remember, Dick? Even Merrill O'Connor was expected, and he never came to student parties, thought they were beneath him or some bullshit. So we're standing around the fire—always something hypnotic about a fire, isn't there?—cups of beer in hand. Some folks were drinking stronger stuff. A couple of joints were being passed around, too. It was that kind of party.

"At some point I realized that the dog was at my side, leaning into me, you know how dogs do to show their affection. Where he'd been since the day I fed him I couldn't say, but he was back, and happily accepted a hot dog from me. It was right about then that you showed up, Dick, you and Beth together. I'd had my eye on her for a while. Smart, pretty, fantastic writer, what's not to like? But that was the first clue I had that you two were an item. Came as quite a surprise, because I didn't think you were really in her league, you know?

"So Beth comes over to me and kisses me on the cheek, pats the dog on his head, and then you take a step toward me like you might shake my hand, and the dog lunges. I mean an angry, barking leap like he thought you were the devil incarnate. Do you remember that, Dick?"

"I remember," I said.

"And that's when Beth said, after we got the dog off you and placated you with a beer, 'that dog is worse than Sam Pluck.'"

"Wait," Charlotte said. "Sam Pluck the serial killer?"

"That's right," I said. "We'd just been talking about him in the car on the way out to Angus's place. Beth had this strange fascination with serial killers. Should have been my first clue she'd be trouble. Anyway, Pluck's crimes were particularly gruesome because he chopped up his victims and turned them into soup."

"So the name kind of stuck," Angus said. "Good ol' Pluck the dog."

We sank into a deepening silence, Angus with his memories of the serial killer dog, me with my failed marriage, Charlotte and Jackson, no doubt, wishing they were elsewhere, except it was their house and they had nowhere to go.

"How is Beth doing?" Angus asked.

Charlotte had risen and was clearing the dinner plates. I saw her shake her head, a warning to Angus, I thought, not to go there.

"As if you don't know," I said.

"Who wants dessert?" Jackson asked, jumping up from the table.

"Trouble in paradise?" Angus asked. "I'm only surprised she stuck with you this long."

Jackson had returned with an apple tart and had begun to cut slices. I stood.

"None for me," I said. "I'd best be getting back."

"That's right, Dick. Run away. Isn't that what you always do? You couldn't stand up to a scrawny mutt and you can't take a bad review. I shouldn't be surprised Beth tossed your ass out or that you'd show up in this backwater to lick your wounds. No offense, Char."

Charlotte, at the sink and her back to us, raised her hand dismissively, having, apparently, heard every word. Jackson, weighing his own options, retreated from the table, wisely taking the cake knife with him.

It was ridiculous and Angus had a good fifty pounds on me so a physical altercation was out of the question, but I leaned across the table hoping to seem threatening.

"Listen to me, you son of a bitch, you never stood a chance with Beth. I can't tell you how many times she called you a pompous ass. And we both laughed out loud when that derivative story collection came out—"

"That won the Pulitzer? That one?"

"—because they reminded us of the drivel you passed off as innovative back at Iowa, still the same old horseshit in a new wrapper, just like everything you've ever written."

Charlotte reappeared, hands up as if she thought she needed to separate us before we came to blows. "Now, boys."

"Not to worry, Charlotte. I'm leaving. Thank you for a lovely dinner." I grabbed my coat and headed outside, steaming, and flung myself into my car.

If this were a novel, I thought as the engine warmed up, I'd rush back in there and punch Angus in the nose. Instead of retreating from the confrontation, I'd give the reader a real climax, where the protagonist and the antagonist duke it out. None of this step back and live to fight another day bullshit. Angus was right about that. That's how it's always been. I surrendered to the fucking dog, the dentist, and now Angus.

Heat had begun to fill the car. I sat with my hands on the wheel, watching snow flurries drift into the headlight beams. Is that what should happen next? Should I do what I should have done decades ago?

But it wasn't a novel and, besides, Angus meant nothing to me. It was an old conflict, one that no longer mattered, if it ever did. No, I wouldn't storm back into the house.

Instead, I took out my phone and listened to Beth's message again. She did sound sincere in her greeting. It was nice of her to call. It was nice to hear her voice. Nice.

THE SCOTTISH PLAY

We've been together for several months now, performing a trio of Shakespeare plays in rotating repertory at venues all over the Midwest. One night we're at a senior center in Indianapolis performing *The Tempest* for white-haired ladies in wheelchairs who titter at the appearance of Caliban, played by a muscular young actor who insisted on doing the part shirtless, and the next we're at a community college in Peoria doing *Love's Labour's Lost* for a bunch of college kids who've come only because they've been promised extra credit. The students slouch in their seats, barely paying attention, until the dynamic Princess of France arrives to stir things up. It's fun to see that change come over them.

Every audience presents its own challenge, but we always have a blast trying to breathe life into plays that have been around for four hundred years and that too many people encounter only in dusty books and required courses in high school. One way we do that is by keeping the houselights up and engaging directly with the audience, no matter how uncomfortable it might make them. Sometimes that's just a matter of addressing an aside to the bald guy in the third row, making him squirm a little, but when we do *The Tempest*, Ariel flits and dances through the crowd, peeking into women's purses or under their chairs, much to everyone's amusement. It always gets a big laugh. When you come to one of our performances, you've got to pay attention or you'll end up being part of the action.

It's been a long tour, but it's coming to an end now. Some of us have signed on for another tour, with three new plays to learn, but others will move on to different gigs elsewhere, and still others have decided that the itinerant actor's life is not for them.

Despite occasional tensions, we've grown really close, as you might expect for twelve actors who spend all day every day with each other. We're a team, pulling together for a common purpose. One downside to that is there's never an opportunity to be alone, except in the bathroom, and even then there's a chance someone will walk in on you while you're doing your business. That much togetherness can wear on you, as it has on us.

For one thing, the non-profit theater that hired us doesn't have a lot of money, so we have to share motel rooms on the road. Most of us are young, not too far removed from college, and don't mind having roommates. Officially, because we're eight men and four women, we're assigned same-sex roommates, and the numbers work out. But there are always complications. There's a married couple in our troupe this year, so naturally they get to room together, which leaves us with odd numbers for the other pairings. Most of the guys wouldn't object to sharing with the women, but management is reluctant to force anyone to do it. Currently, there is no problem because the body-builder who plays Caliban has hooked up with our ingenue, the very pretty and amazingly talented woman who plays Miranda in *The Tempest*. Their scenes together in that show are incredibly moving if you know that they're sleeping together in real life. And during the pre-show music we perform, they have a beautiful duet of "Falling Slowly" that never fails to make the audience quiet down and listen. Some of the other relationships—including between a couple of the guys in the troupe—have been shorter lived and rather volatile. As we said: complications.

We've been doing these plays now for many months, and we could probably perform them in our sleep. Our director warns us about this because it can, understandably, lead to some pretty dead performances. She tries to keep us on our toes, though. Once, during a performance of *LLL*, in the middle of the crucial scene where the Princess of France is lecturing Navarre, a scene that was falling flat and in danger of stupefying the audience, a rubber chicken flew out of the wings and landed at Navarre's feet. That got a stunned laugh from the huge group of high-schoolers in attendance— totally inappropriate at that moment in the play—and nods of awareness from the members of the company who were on stage at the time. We knew we were just phoning it in, and from then on we brought a new intensity to the performance. All's well that ends well.

One night we were performing our third play of the rotation, *Macbeth*, one that we get asked to do a lot because it's so well known. In our introduction before the show we do a comic bit to explain why there's a superstition in the theater world about mentioning the name of the play. One of the cast members begins to utter the name and another stops her and says, "You mean, 'The Scottish Play.'" She accepts the correction and then keeps going. Eventually she gets to the point where she's about to say the name again and the other actor interrupts. The audience always chuckles at that. When it happens the third time, the audience is full-throated in their laughter, and they're in hysterics when it happens a fourth time. At which point we explain the superstition—the curse on the play. We're not sure what sort of disaster is supposed to befall us if the name is uttered aloud, but it makes for a nice takeaway for uninitiated audiences to learn from the production.

Before the action of the play began that night, our stage manager informed us that a woman with a service dog would be seated in the front row. When we do the show on a normal proscenium stage, it's harder to engage with the audience in the way we like because they're below us and separated from the action by the orchestra pit. It's much better on a thrust stage or a black box theater, or even in a makeshift space with folding chairs that can be set up in any configuration. In this instance we'd been booked into a community center's reception hall, with chairs arranged on three sides and our discovery space—a portable curtain and backdrop through which we make most of our entrances and exits—at the rear. During the pre-show music, we noticed the woman and her service dog, sitting stage right. The dog was on a mat at her feet, head resting on its paws, and the woman was chatting with an older lady next to her. Her mother, maybe? We've played to dogs before, and last year when we did *Two Gentlemen of Verona* we used a dog in the cast to play the part of Crab the dog. That was fun. A challenge, but fun. So there's a dog in the front row. No big deal.

At the conclusion of the introduction, which tonight was delivered by our body-builder/ingenue couple who in this play have the roles of MacDuff and his wife, he says, "We hope you enjoy this evening's performance of Macbeth," and she shoots him a dirty look, like "What have you done?" That elicits one last chuckle from the audience, who then settle in to be entertained.

The play begins as usual with the three witches, the Weird Sisters, entering through the rear curtain. "When shall we three meet again, in thunder, lightning, or in rain?" They're quite a sight, those witches, with costumes that make them look like they're draped with seaweed and slime. Plus, there's the noise of the thunder and lightning and their high-pitched voices, all of which puts the audience on edge and also gets the dog's attention. He lifts his head, tilts it to one side in that puzzled expression dogs get. No problem. Some of the kids in the audience have the same look on their faces.

Then the witches vanish back behind the curtain, reappearing in Scene 3 when they're encountered by Macbeth and Banquo who are on their way home after vanquishing the rebel Macdonwald. They hear the Weird Sisters' improbable prophesies about their futures and then, after the witches vanish again, news arrives that the first prediction, that Macbeth will be named Thane of Cawdor, has come true. This sets Macbeth's mind racing and he muses aloud in an aside: "Cannot be ill, cannot be good: if ill, why hath it given me earnest of success, commencing in a truth? I am thane of Cawdor." He's getting the idea that the second prediction, that he'll be named King of Scotland, might also come true. Ambition burns in his eyes.

Our casting director did a great job with these plays. Our Macbeth is a veteran actor named Carl who looks just the way Macbeth should look. He's tall and powerfully built, with a salt-and-pepper beard that makes him appear both fierce and regal and also just a little bit murderous. He's been around the block a few times, Carl has. You should have seen him in Lear last season. Magnificent.

Anyway, as Macbeth turns away from Banquo and the messenger to deliver the aside, the woman in the front row with the service dog stands up. We hear a collective gasp from the audience. Wait, though, is this a part of the show? Has the company planted another Weird Sister in the audience? We're known for pulling stunts like that, so could it be?

But no, we've done nothing of the kind. This isn't supposed to happen. The woman approaches Macbeth, her arms extended in sympathy for his dilemma as if she wants to give him a hug. The dog is sitting up now, alert, and we can see the confused look in his eyes. What am I supposed to do when this happens? They never taught us this in Service Dog School! Macbeth is cool, though, that Carl is a real pro, and he guides the woman back to her seat, all the while continuing his aside: "If chance will have me king, why, chance may crown me, without my stir." The scene comes to an end and Macbeth and Banquo exit through the rear curtain. The audience breathes a sigh of relief, but that's nothing compared to the look on Carl's face as he joins us backstage: What the fuck?

The play goes on without incident, although we all keep an eye on the woman and her dog, and we redirect some of our asides and audience address to stage left, lest she view the interaction as an invitation to join another scene. We see that her friends have their hands on her, keeping her in her seat.

Macbeth goes home, his wife gets all excited about the prospect of his becoming King, and they prepare to welcome Duncan, the current King, to their castle. Lady Macbeth is a stunner in every way. She's played by Cassandra—Cassie to us—who is classically trained and has a voice that can be heard in the next county. She's tall, with long, shimmering brown hair that looks very ladylike, but can also be teased into the crazy look that works later in the play. In this scene, she oozes ambition. If Carl's Macbeth is clearly on the fence about killing Duncan—a balancing act that is hard for an actor to pull off but Carl gets just right—there is no doubt about Cassie's Lady Macbeth. She wants it, and she wants it bad.

The audience becomes rapt now, as Duncan retires to his bedchamber and Macbeth is faced with doing the deed. Even those who know what's coming next hang on every word: "Is this a dagger which I see before me, the handle toward my hand?"

But then we notice the woman. She's on her feet again and so is the dog. "Come let me clutch thee. I have thee not, and yet I see thee still." Carl is at center stage delivering these lines as the woman approaches. This time the audience knows it's not part of the play and that something is seriously amiss. And Carl may be a seasoned actor, but nobody can be prepared for this kind of thing. He moves hesitantly toward stage right, although the blocking calls for him to move the opposite direction. The woman and the dog come closer. Why don't her companions jump up to rein her in?

She grabs Macbeth's arm with both hands, as if she's pleading with him not to kill Duncan, and Carl falls completely out of character.

"What the hell are you doing, lady?" Carl shouts. The audience shifts uncomfortably in their seats.

The woman drops her arms and a stricken look comes over her face as if she's been in a trance, has suddenly awoken, and has no idea where she is. The dog senses something is wrong and barks nervously. The woman doesn't move, so Carl, with one eye on the watchful dog, nudges her back toward her chair. Finally, her seatmates stand to take control of her as she sits. The dog resumes his spot next to her. Carl gives her a look—it's a warning, sure, but compassionate, too, because obviously there's something off with this woman—urging her to stay put this time.

Carl returns to center stage. "Now, where was I?" he says, and the audience applauds. He's Macbeth again when he returns to the top of his monologue and says, "Is this a dagger which I see before me?"

The danger has passed, but backstage we're nervous. In just a minute, Macbeth is going to kill Duncan and emerge on stage with his hands covered in blood. Is that going to set the woman off again? Or the dog? What will happen when Lady Macbeth goes nuts and sinks to the stage trying to wash her hands clean: "Out, damned spot! Out, I say!" Mercifully, though, our stage manager rings the bell signaling that it's time for intermission. The first half has not gone well, but the audience applauds politely and stands to stretch their legs.

The woman's companions have come to their senses and usher her and the dog out of the performance space. They're putting on their coats, so it's clear they're actually leaving and not just taking a break. Our stage manager speaks to them as they go and he's obviously relieved. Maybe we can get back on track for the second half.

The bell rings to indicate we're about to get started again, and sure enough the woman's seat is empty. The dog is gone. We resume.

Act IV begins with the Weird Sisters gathered around their steaming pot. Everybody loves this scene, and usually the witches really ham it up. "Double, double, toil and trouble; fire burn and cauldron bubble." Tonight, though, as the second witch begins tossing ingredients into the pot and reciting the recipe for the witches' brew, something seems off kilter. "Fillet of a fenny snake, in the cauldron boil and bake; eye of newt and toe of frog, wool of bat and tongue of dog."

At the word "dog," the audience turns en masse to look at the empty chair where the woman had been with her loyal friend. Eye of newt is one thing, but tongue of dog?

The audience reaction has stopped the second witch cold. It's unlikely that she's forgotten the next line, considering how many times we've performed this play, and yet there's an awkward silence. The third witch gamely moves on: "Scale of dragon, tooth of wolf." Now she, too, stops. What's come over them? The next thing that's supposed to happen is Hecate's appearance, but he's nowhere to be found and misses his cue.

We have both a director and a stage manager, and we might expect them to step in and take charge of this catastrophe, but they've been AWOL since the intermission. We think about sending Cassie—Lady Macbeth—to find them before the whole production goes down in flames, but we're afraid we'll lose her, too.

The audience is restless, wondering what the hell is going on, but Carl, veteran that he is, assumes command. It isn't quite time for his entrance, but he runs on stage anyway, skipping ahead a bit to his line, "How now, you secret, black and midnight hags!"

This scene is crucial because in it Macbeth learns—or thinks he learns—that he's invincible against MacDuff's forces. There are loopholes that he doesn't understand until later, but it's a great setup for the final twists that make this play so powerful. However, the apparitions who deliver this information to him— the actors who also play Duncan, MacDuff, and MacDuff's wife wearing masks and ghostly costumes—fail to enter. At this point, though, nothing will surprise Carl, so he turns their revelations into an impromptu soliloquy that anyone familiar with the text would find highly unusual. He's about to wrap up the scene, alone on stage—"Time, though anticipatest my dread exploits: the flighty purpose never is o'ertook unless the deed go with it"—when the woman we thought had left comes down the center aisle, trailed by her dog.

Carl looks past the woman for her companions, no doubt hoping they'll stop her before she reaches the stage, but she keeps coming, like the marching trees of Birnam Wood that will eventually lead to Macbeth's doom. She steps up to him, the dog at her heels, and puts her arms around him, resting her head on his shoulder. The dog sits and looks up at them. The audience watches, spellbound.

"Oh, hell," Carl says, extracting himself from the woman's embrace. "Someone ring the damn bell," he shouts to the heavens, then runs upstage to disappear behind the curtain. From somewhere backstage someone, probably Carl himself, rings the bell to signal that this performance has ended. The bell is muted and faint, but the audience, with all of their attention focused on the woman and her dog, applauds.

We have never ended a show without a curtain call, but tonight no one emerges on stage to receive their due. At first, the clapping is tepid, the audience still unsure about what they've witnessed, but gradually it builds and becomes thunderous. They cheer. The high school students stomp their feet and whistle. The rest of the audience rises, applauding enthusiastically, for a standing ovation.

The woman and her puzzled dog are alone at center stage. She turns to face the audience. She smiles and takes a bow.

Author's Note

If you're looking at this page, thank you! Seriously, anyone who is interested in books, and my book in particular, has my gratitude!

More specifically, I'd like to thank the editors of the magazines in whose pages many of these stories first appeared. As you may note on the acknowledgments page at the front of this book, some of the stories were written and published more than a decade ago. I'm thrilled to have the opportunity for the stories to find new readers.

Many of these stories, especially the more recent ones, were written during residencies at the Virginia Center for the Creative Arts, a heavenly retreat providing the time and space to create for artists in all disciplines. I'm grateful for the time I've spent there.

Finally, thanks once again to Kevin Morgan Watson at Press 53 for his support and encouragement and for bringing this book to life.

Clifford Garstang is the author of a novel, *The Shaman of Turtle Valley*, a novel in stories, *What the Zhang Boys Know*, which won the Library of Virginia Award for Fiction, and a prize-winning short story collection, *In an Uncharted Country*. He is also the editor of *Everywhere Stories: Short Fiction from a Small Planet*, an anthology series of stories set around the world, and the co-founder and former editor of *Prime Number Magazine*.

Garstang's work has appeared in *Bellevue Literary Review, Blackbird, Cream City Review, The Hopkins Review, Los Angeles Review, Shenandoah, Tampa Review, Virginia Quarterly Review*, and elsewhere, and has received Distinguished Mention in the Best American Series. He has won the *Confluence* Fiction Prize and the *GSU Review* Fiction Prize and has been awarded fellowships by the Virginia Center for the Creative Arts, Ragdale Foundation, Hambidge Center for the Arts, and the Sewanee Writers' Conference. He is the recipient of an Indiana Emerging Author Award and an Emerging Writer Fellowship from the Writer's Center in Maryland.

After receiving a BA in Philosophy from Northwestern University, Garstang served as a Peace Corps Volunteer in

South Korea, where he taught English at Jonbuk University. He then earned an MA in English and a JD, *magna cum laude*, both from Indiana University. He practiced international law in Chicago, Los Angeles, and Singapore with one of the largest law firms in the United States. He earned a Master of Public Administration degree from Harvard University's John F. Kennedy School of Government and worked for Harvard Law School's Program on International Financial Systems as a legal reform consultant in Almaty, Kazakhstan. He then served as Senior Counsel for East Asia at the World Bank in Washington, DC, where his work focused on China, Vietnam, Korea, and Indonesia. Subsequently he earned an MFA in Creative Writing from Queens University of Charlotte. He currently lives in the Shenandoah Valley of Virginia.

www.ingramcontent.com/pod-product-compliance
Lightning Source LLC
Chambersburg PA
CBHW031237260626
4/169CB00007B/2341

* 9 7 8 1 9 5 0 4 1 3 1 8 8 *